Amish Christmas Mystery

Ettie Smith Amish Mysteries Book 10

Samantha Price

ISBN 978-1540445834

Chapter 1

Elderly Amish widow Ettie Smith looked up from her needlework and stared at her older sister. They often sat together in the living room in silence while Ettie did her needlework and Elsa-May knitted.

"This might be our last Christmas together."

"Why, where are you going?" Elsa-May asked without missing one purl or one plain.

"I don't plan on going anywhere, but we're both older than most people we know, now that everyone else around your age and mine is dead. Other than the meetings, all we do these days is go to funerals of people younger than us."

"We won't have a choice about that. When *Gott* calls us home, it's our time to go."

"I'm simply saying it might be our last Christmas together."

"You say that every year and yet here we are, still alive and kicking on another Christmas Eve.

Neither of us look like we're about to take our last breath."

"One of these years I'm going to be right! And if it's not this year it could be the next!" Ettie gave a sharp nod of her head as though she'd somehow proved her point.

Elsa-May dropped her knitting into her lap and looked over the top of her knitting glasses. "What's your point, Ettie? You usually have one when you prattle on like this."

"I was just wondering if you got me a Christmas present."

"Nee, nothing. We never get each other a gift for Christmas—not since we were young."

That wasn't quite true. Every year Ettie had gotten Elsa-May something and gotten nothing in return. "I'd like you to get me something this Christmas because it might..."

"Be our last together?" Elsa-May asked.

"That's right."

Elsa-May finished her row, and while one hand held her knitting, the other pushed her spectacles onto her forehead pushing back her prayer *kapp*. "And what is it you'd like for this Christmas present?"

Ettie pressed her lips together so tight they formed a straight line. "Nothing if you're going to speak like that."

Elsa-May rolled her eyes. "I was just asking a question. Do you have your mind set on something, or am I supposed to guess? You know Christmas is not very important to me."

"Why can't you ever get into the Christmas spirit and have some fun?"

Elsa-May huffed. "Giving presents, and talk of Christmas is for the young. It wasn't really the day that Jesus was born anyway. They've proven that. We should celebrate Jesus' birth every day of the year not just on one day."

Ettie knew all Elsa-May's talk was simply an effort to throw her off the track about getting her a present. "It doesn't matter whether it's the right day or not. It's the day people choose to celebrate His birth, so isn't it good that people do that tomorrow rather than not do it at all?" Ettie leaned forward waiting for her sister's reply.

"I guess so. You do have a point. What does it have to do with a gift, though?"

Ettie shook her head. "Never mind."

"What? Are you saying you don't want one now?"

"That's right." Ettie picked up her sewing and jabbed the needle into the sampler while Elsa-May breathed out heavily.

"Let's go to the store, then. We'll buy each other a gift, but only this once. Next year and the ones after that, we'll make each other something."

Ettie's face lit up. "Do you mean it?" Ettie could barely keep the smile from her face. And this *could* very well be their last. Elsa-May was likely to go first with her health issues, Ettie figured, and a gift would give Ettie something to look back on if Elsa-May wasn't with her at the next Christmas.

"Well?" Elsa-May asked.

"It's your turn to speak. I asked you if you meant it?"

"*Jah.* I never say things I don't mean."

"Let's go." Ettie watched Elsa-May's eyes flicker to the gray sky out the window and then to Snowy, her small white fluffy dog who was curled up close to the fire in the corner of the room. "Leave him inside," Ettie said.

"I intended to." After she'd placed the knitting in the bag by her feet, Elsa-May pushed herself out of her chair. "We'll leave the dog door open so he can go out and do his business."

"I don't think he'll even know we're gone. He's been sleeping a lot lately."

"Must be the cold."

"*Jah.* We should be sure to wear some warm clothes in case it snows."

Ettie walked to her bedroom to get ready for their visit to the stores. It would be busy at the shops, and cold outdoors. When her husband had been alive, they had big family Christmas dinners where everyone would exchange gifts. Now he was gone, and most of her children had their own families to look after, and now she had great grandchildren.

All of her children had stayed within the Amish community and made good marriages except for two of her daughters, Myra and Deborah.

Ettie hadn't spoken to either of her daughters for years. Both resented Ettie for raising them in the Amish community. It was as though they thought she'd been born into the Amish herself and married an Amish man, had children and raised them in the community simply to ruin their lives. They could choose when they came of age, and Myra and Deborah had both chosen to leave.

Myra had gotten into a spot of bother a few years back and had contacted her, but after that was resolved she'd not kept in contact.

Christmas was a sad time for Ettie. She'd gone from being a central person in her children's lives to being someone on the outer fringes. Although all her children—apart from Myra and Deborah—and their offspring respected her, she was no longer the most important person in their lives. This situation never usually bothered her, but at this time of the year, her mind often drifted to days gone by.

Ettie whipped off her dressing gown and pulled on her dress as quickly as she could to keep out the cold. It was hard to get out of her warm dressing gown on chilly days when they were only going to stay at home. After she pulled on two pairs of black stockings, her apron, cape and lastly her prayer *kapp,* she headed out to the living room to find her black over-bonnet.

Waiting for her by the front door was Elsa-May, fully dressed and ready to go.

"You were fast," Ettie said.

"I was dressed. I just had to put a warmer layer on."

"Maybe while we're out we can get some extra-special food for tomorrow?"

"Why? It'll only be just us, won't it?"

"Jah, but we can still have something nice to eat for the midday meal."

They'd both been invited to Elsa-May's grandson's house for a big family Christmas dinner.

"If that's what will make you happy, Ettie."

"Well, it'll help. And it'll also help if you try to

be excited by it being this time of year. Everyone is celebrating and happy."

Elsa-May put her two forefingers either side of her mouth and stretched them up toward her ears to make a smile.

Ettie laughed. "That's much better. Now stay like that until tomorrow night."

Elsa-May opened the front door and a freezing draft of air swept through the house. "Are you certain you want to go out?"

"*Jah.* And I want to come back and make candies and cookies to take with us tomorrow night."

"I'd forgotten all about that."

Ettie tapped a finger on her head. "Up here for thinking."

Both women stepped out of the house, closed the door behind them and hurried down the road to the shanty that housed the phone that everyone on their street used. From there, they would call for a taxi to take them to town.

* * *

Ettie woke up on Christmas morning pleased that she'd reached the milestone of another Christmas day. Normally she would've stayed wrapped in her dressing down for a good part of the morning, but today she swiftly changed out of her nightdress, ready for a hearty breakfast.

When she sat across from Elsa-May, she asked, "Will we open them now?"

When they had gone shopping the day before, they'd gone in different directions so one could not see what the other was purchasing. In Ettie's opinion the best part of a gift was the surprise.

Elsa-May raised an eyebrow as she poured a cup of tea for herself from the teapot. "Do what?"

"Open our presents now."

"Why not wait until tonight before we go to Jeremiah and Ava's?"

"Are they expecting us? I never said I was going," Ettie said.

"They're having a lot of people over there tonight so they won't miss us if we're not there. They said they'd expect us if they saw us. I'd like us to go, though. It's better than staying home and seeing no one for the whole of Christmas day."

Ettie sighed. Staying home would suit her perfectly with the weather as cold as it had been. "We've had so many invitations between Christmas and New Year it's been hard to know which ones to take."

Elsa-May nodded. "As much as I love the great *grosskin* I don't know if I could take all that crying and all that ruckus at my age."

Ettie giggled. "That's the best thing about being as old as we are, we're not expected to do anything. We can always say we're too tired."

"And that would be true," Elsa-May said raising the teacup to her lips.

"Well?" Ettie nodded to the two brightly wrapped presents commanding attention in the center of the table.

Elsa-May stared at the gifts. "Do you want to open yours first?"

"*Nee,* I want to see your face first before I open mine."

"Okay." Elsa-May pushed her half eaten plate of eggs aside, reached out and took her present. She ripped the red and green paper open to reveal a set of knitting needles, a pattern and brown wool. Her eyebrows rose as she picked up the paper pattern.

"It's for me," Ettie explained.

Elsa-May's head shot up. "What do you mean it's for you? It's my gift."

"The finished product will be a shawl for me so I can sit and do my needlework and have a warm soft shawl around my shoulders to keep me nice and cozy."

Elsa-May's upper lip curled with disapproval. "Your present to me is something that I have to knit for you?"

"That's right," Ettie said smiling.

"How is that a gift for me?"

"You're always making things for other people. And for the great *grosskin,* so I thought you would like to make something for me before your arthritis spreads further."

Elsa-May dropped the wool and the pattern onto

the table. "How thoughtful of you."

"I knew you'd like it." Ettie reached out her hand and touched the soft brown wool. "Normally I don't like the color brown, but this was so soft I couldn't resist it."

Elsa-May kept silent.

"Shall I open mine now?" Ettie asked when she looked across at Elsa-May.

Her sister gave a sweep of her hand. "Go ahead."

Ettie was delighted. "It's lovely paper." Ettie stared at the bright gold Christmas bells on the dark green background.

"I hope you like what's inside just as well as the paper."

"I'm sure I will." After she took the gift into her hands, she pulled the paper away to reveal tissue paper. Inside was a china cup, saucer, and plate set; Ettie could tell that by the shape of it. She carefully peeled the tissue paper away and saw it. "It's beautiful." She stared at the pale green set with the pink rosebuds as she set the plate down first, then the saucer and lastly set the cup onto the saucer. "It's quite possibly the prettiest thing I've ever seen."

"I'm glad you like it."

"I do. *Denke.* Can I use it now?"

"Whenever you like. It's yours." Elsa-May then murmured, "Unlike my present."

Ettie ignored her sister's comment. She always found something to complain about. Once she started knitting, Ettie was sure Elsa-May would appreciate the gift and then when she was finished, she'd have the appreciation of seeing Ettie in the shawl. Ettie took the cup over to the sink and rinsed it out, then sat back down to pour herself a cup of tea. She brought the cup to her lips and took a sip. "It tastes much better in this cup."

"Good. I'm glad."

Ettie looked at the pile of wool on the table. "I'm glad you like your present."

Elsa-May drew her lips together as she stared at the wool.

"You don't have to start on it today. Tomorrow will do," Ettie said.

Elsa-May chuckled and Ettie smiled at the delight on her sister's face. If her present gave Elsa-May such delight, she'd have to give her more like that.

After Elsa-May and Ettie had finished washing up the morning dishes, Ettie asked, "Are we going to Jeremiahs or not?"

"I've had so much joy from your present, I don't think I could take any more Christmas cheer."

"So we're not going?" Ettie asked.

"I think I'll be happy enough to stay home."

"Me too. I'm happy to stay home in front of the fire. Maybe we'll get some visitors dropping by."

"Weren't you going to make some candy and cake? That would be useful in case we get some people stopping by like we normally do."

"Okay. I'll get started on them now."

"I'll help you."

"Goodie!" Ettie rolled up her sleeves to get started. There was always excitement and happiness in the air at Christmas time. "I'm glad you like your present."

"Well, it's hardly *my* present is it?"

Ettie stared at her sister. "What do you mean?"

"You gave me a present that I have to knit, and then when I'm finished it, I have to hand it over to you."

"Jah, that's right. I know how you like knitting."

Elsa-May's gaze fell to the floor and then she looked at the ceiling as she shook her head.

"What was that look for?" Ettie asked. Now she was confused. A minute ago, Elsa-May was acting like she loved her present and now Ettie didn't know what she thought of it.

Just as Elsa-May had her mouth open to speak, there was a knock at the door.

"I wonder who this could be," Ettie remarked as she took a step toward the door.

"It could be Ava come to see if we're going tonight."

Ettie, nearly at the door, called over her shoulder, "I think she would be too busy preparing for her guests to come and see if we're coming." Once Ettie had pulled the door open, she saw her estranged daughter, Myra, standing there with a plate of food in her hands.

"Hello, Mother. I hope you don't mind that I've come early."

Ettie stood still with her mouth gaping open. She hadn't seen Myra for years.

"Close your mouth, Mother, or you'll catch flies. Well, are you going to let me in or what?"

Ettie closed her mouth and stepped aside to allow her daughter inside.

Elsa-May hurried over to her. "Myra, it's so good to see you. This is a surprise."

"You didn't think I'd come?"

"Nee, I didn't."

Myra passed Ettie the food, while Elsa-May helped Myra out of her coat.

"What's this?" Ettie asked looking down at the food.

"Just food. Don't worry, it's something that I bought. I didn't actually cook it. That's just another reason I'm so different. I hate cooking. I would've never made a good Amish woman. Are you sure I wasn't adopted?" Myra gave a small laugh.

"Nee, I had too many *kinner* to think about adopting more."

"That's a pity. It would've been the only thing to have made sense."

Elsa-May hung Myra's coat on one of the pegs by the front door.

Ettie stared at the brightly-colored flowing dress that her daughter was wearing. It was certainly a change from the business suits she wore when they were last in touch.

"You're both well?" Myra asked as she sat down on the couch.

"Jah, we've both been keeping well. Elsa-May has a spot of bother with arthritis in her hands and then she has…"

"Don't speak in Pennsylvania Dutch to me, Mother. It brings back bad memories, and it's already all I can do to come here."

Ettie pushed her lips together. "I only said a couple of words."

"Also, Ettie, Myra didn't come here to listen to what's wrong with me health wise."

As she sat on the couch next to her daughter, Ettie wondered why Myra was there. Ettie was pleased to see her but she was acting like they should've been expecting her.

Elsa-May continued, "We always like to see you, Myra, but I have to wonder, why are you here?"

"I came for a Christmas party that I'd never forget. Mind you, Mother, I was quite surprised to get that note from you and I'm willing to hear what you have to say."

Ettie glared at Elsa-May. Had her sister written a note pretending it was from her? What was Elsa-May doing meddling in her relationship with her daughter? She'd never stuck her nose in before. They'd always kept out of one another's business.

"When is everyone else arriving?" Myra asked.

When Ettie opened her mouth to say something, there was another knock on the door.

Ettie only wished that Elsa-May had let her in on her plans.

Chapter 2

Ettie opened her front door and was most surprised to see Naomi Fuller standing there with a casserole dish in her hands.

She held out the dish toward Ettie. "Am I too early?" Naomi asked.

"Um, I don't think so," Ettie said, glancing over her shoulder. "Come in."

Naomi passed the casserole dish to Ettie and then walked in the door.

"You sit with the others in the living room, Naomi, while I put this in the kitchen."

Once Ettie got to the kitchen, she stayed there trying to work out what was happening. Had she invited people and forgotten?

She heard Myra and Naomi greeting each other. They would've remembered each other from when they'd been young girls together.

"Mother, what are you doing?"

Ettie looked around to see Myra standing in the

doorway of the kitchen with hands on hips.

"I'm just putting the casserole in the oven to keep it warm until we're ready to eat."

"That's not what I meant," Myra hissed. "I didn't think you'd be having too many other people over; certainly not people from the community. When are we going to get a chance to have that talk?"

"Elsa-May and I *are* from the community."

"That's different. I thought you wanted the two of us to sort out our differences." Myra raised her eyebrows, and added, "One of us owes the other an apology."

"Neither of us has ever agreed on exactly who owes whom that apology. Why would today be different?"

"Well, why am I here? Do you think that we'll come to some common ground without an apology?"

Before Ettie could answer, there was another knock on the door.

"I'll get it," Elsa-May called out from the living room.

"Just how many people did you invite, Mother?" Myra spoke through gritted teeth.

Ettie shrugged her shoulders. If she told her it was Elsa-May who'd invited her, this might ruin her last chance to have Myra back in her life. "I don't remember," Ettie said.

"Just as I suspected, you're losing your mind. I had hoped that you were finally ready to reconcile and apologize for my lost youth, but I guess I was wrong. You've got no idea what you're doing."

Ettie was upset at her daughter, but was distracted when Myra closed her eyes and took deliberate slow breaths. "Are you alright, Myra?"

"I'm trying not to get angry because it's not good for my aura. It fragments and changes color with stress."

"We wouldn't want that," Ettie said, wondering if she'd heard Myra correctly.

"Ettie!"

Ettie looked over at Elsa-May who'd stuck her head around the kitchen door. "What is it?"

"Why did you invite Moses Stoll and Naomi

Fuller here—both at the same time? The two of them are reminded of bad things when they're together. Don't you remember?"

"Nee."

Elsa-May stepped closer. "That's hardly a response."

Ettie bit her lip. "Can you excuse us a moment, Myra?"

Myra threw up her hands and left the room in a huff.

Ettie glared at her sister. "Why are you making out I invited the people? Is that your plan, for Myra and me to make amends? You could've told me about it at least."

Elsa-May huffed. "If you wanted to be around people we could've gone to Jeremiah's *haus.*"

"I wanted to, but you didn't!"

Elsa-May shook her head. "That's not what you said before! We're hardly prepared for all these guests. I suppose it's just as well that they all brought food."

There was another knock at the door.

"How many people did you invite, Ettie?" asked Elsa-May in shock.

Ettie glared back at Elsa-May. "I thought it was you who invited them. Didn't you invite Myra here to force us to speak to one another?"

"*Nee.* Are you certain that you didn't."

"*Nee! Jah,* I mean. I'm certain that I didn't."

"Why are they all coming here?"

"I have no idea!"

"I better go and see who's at the door this time."

Elsa-May hurried out to open the front door while Myra came back into the kitchen.

"What's going on, Mother?" Myra asked.

Just as Ettie had opened her mouth to answer, yet another knock sounded on the door.

"It appears we're having a few people for dinner."

Half an hour later, the kitchen table was covered in food and the living room was crowded with people.

"Ettie, are you sure you didn't do this?" Elsa-

May asked as they both stared at all the food on the table.

"I already told you I didn't do anything."

"How could you invite all these people without letting me know?"

"Elsa-May, do you think you invited them and forgot about it? Believe me, I know nothing about this."

Myra entered the kitchen. "Mother, before you drop dead of a heart attack, I must tell you that I've invited two men to come here tonight. I hope that's okay with you. I'm in a serious relationship and I want to be with him on Christmas night. He said he might come. You'd like him, he's keen for you and me to reconcile."

"That's okay," Ettie said nodding. "He's welcome. Who's the other man?"

"He's a man who's caused me a lot of trouble. He used to be in the community. His name is Earl Fuller."

"Not Naomi's husband?"

Myra's fingertips flew to her mouth. "Oh no. I

forgot that he married someone in the community before he left."

Ettie leaned in and whispered, "Not only that, Myra, Earl ran away with a young girl from the community, leaving poor Naomi alone."

"Jah," Elsa-May added. "I don't know if he'll be welcome here. Ettie and I shouldn't have him in the house. He ran away with young Betsy Stoll and she never came back to the community. Oh dear, and Betsy Stoll's father, Moses, is here tonight, too."

"I didn't even stop to think about all that. I just thought that Christmas would be a perfect time to make amends between Earl and myself. We've had a huge upheaval business wise. I had planned to tell him I'm no longer going to contest that the idea was his. He can have it and run with it."

"What idea?" Ettie asked.

Myra shook her head. "Never mind. It's a long story. I'll call him and tell him not to come. I'll talk to him another time."

"That's best. Do you have a cell phone?"

"Yes, Mother."

Elsa-May suggested, "It's best you go outside to use it."

When Myra left the kitchen, Elsa-May started at Ettie again. "So are you saying you didn't invite anyone here—no one at all?"

"Why would I do that? I thought we were possibly going to Jeremiah's."

"Well, it wasn't me! Why have they all turned up and brought food?"

"I've got no idea in the world."

The sisters stared at each other and then Ettie's gaze swept over all the food on the table. "At least they brought food with them."

"We might as well start feeding them." Elsa-May began taking the lids off the food. "Ettie, you get the plates and the cutlery. We'll have people file through the kitchen and help themselves. I only hope we have enough plates."

When they were nearly finished doing that, there was another knock on the door.

"I'll go," Ettie said hoping the person on the

other side of the door had thought to bring extra plates with them. When the door opened, she was surprised to see her old friend, the retired Detective Crowley, standing before her.

"Hello, Ronald. Did you get an invitation too?"

"No. I'm sorry if I'm disturbing anything. I was just on my way home from a celebration at the club and I wanted to wish you and Elsa-May a Merry Christmas. Although, I'm not sure that you celebrate Christmas."

Ettie looked over her shoulder at the people crowded into their small home. "It looks like we do this Christmas. Come in. Elsa-May will be pleased to see you. We've got quite a gathering here tonight."

"I won't stay. I don't like to interrupt anything."

"Nonsense. Come inside and get warm."

When Crowley took a step through the door, Ettie suddenly remembered that Myra was in the living room. Crowley and Myra had dated briefly some time ago. She turned to warn him that Myra was in the living room, but it was too late.

Myra bounded to her feet when she saw him and looked pleasantly surprised. "Ronald!"

"Myra!"

The two stood there staring at one another as though there was no one else in the room. Ettie quickly disappeared into the kitchen to tell Elsa-May what was happening.

"Elsa-May!" She grabbed onto Elsa-May's sleeve and pulled her to one side of the kitchen so no one would hear what she said. "Ronald Crowley has just arrived."

"What?"

"Detective Crowley."

"He's here?"

"Jah, he's here, but he didn't get an invitation like the others. He just stopped by to wish us a Merry Christmas. Then I forgot that Myra was in the room. He came in, they saw each other, and they both stood there staring into each other's eyes like two lovesick puppies."

Elsa-May pushed Ettie out of the way, hurried to the door of the kitchen and peeped around the corner. A high-pitched chuckle escaped her lips and she turned around to Ettie. "Who would've thought?"

"Do you think they might rekindle their relationship?" Ettie asked.

"Didn't I hear Myra say she had a boyfriend or something and that he might come here tonight?"

That was typical of Elsa-May; she never missed anything.

"That's right, and she did say that he might be coming here tonight."

"You don't have to repeat everything I say, Ettie."

"I'm sorry. My head's in a muddle. I haven't seen Myra for years and now all this is happening. All these people are here and we don't know why."

Elsa-May took two steps toward Ettie, and patted her on the shoulder. "I'm sorry I'm so bossy sometimes. I don't mean to be."

"That's okay. I'm used to it." Before Elsa-May could say another word, Ettie spoke again. "What's going on here tonight?"

"We need to get to the bottom of this, Ettie."

"Of course we do, but how do we do that?"

"Simple. All we have to do is find out how these people were invited and once we find that out, we'll be closer to knowing the truth of the matter."

"Will we do that before or after we eat?" Ettie asked, looking at the food.

"I don't want to wait another minute longer. Let's see what we can find out now."

"Okay, I'm right behind you."

Ettie pushed Elsa-May out the door first and she followed close behind. Before they could do or say anything, the front door burst open with a gust of wind, and flakes of snow whipped through the door.

When the snow settled, a flush-faced Santa Claus was framed in the doorway. "Help!" he shouted. "There's a dead man!"

Chapter 3

Ettie and Elsa-May stared at the red-suited Santa Claus who sported a long white bushy beard and a red, fur-trimmed hat.

He held his broad stomach as he yelled again, "There's a dead man!" The house fairly shook from his voice.

Crowley was the first to make a move. In no time, he was in front of Santa Claus. "Where?"

"Out there." Santa Claus stepped back and pointed outside.

Crowley ran through the door. Ettie and Elsa-May hurried to look outside. They could make out a dark figure lying halfway through their gate.

"Is he dead?" Ettie asked.

Elsa-May replied, "*Jah,* I'm sure that's what he said. You go out and see what it's all about, Ettie. I'll see if I can find out who invited all these people."

"Will do."

While Ettie slung her black shawl over her shoulders, everyone present returned to their conversations. It seemed that no one believed Santa Claus that there was a dead man outside.

Crowley was now on his phone reporting the incident to the authorities. Ettie could see the man lying on his back in front of her. His body was half in her garden and half on the sidewalk.

Santa Claus was now leaning over the man until Crowley assured him that the man was well and truly dead and that he shouldn't touch anything. Ettie hurried closer to get a better look wondering if she might know the man. When Ettie looked into the man's face, she gasped. She did recognize him. He was older than when she'd seen him last, but she never forgot a face. Names yes, but faces never.

"Do you know him, Ettie?" Crowley asked.

"I do."

A strained voice from over Ettie's shoulder said, "I know him, too."

Ettie swung around to see Myra.

Myra continued coldly, "His name is Earl Fuller.

We grew up in the community together and then we met again recently."

"I'm sorry Ettie, and Myra," Crowley said.

"I feel responsible," Myra said.

Crowley frowned. "And why is that?"

"We had a huge falling out and I asked him here today to try to work things out with him."

Detective Crowley pulled his phone out of his pocket and immediately called in the man's name. When he put his phone back in his pocket, he looked at Santa Claus. "How did you happen to be in this street?"

"I'm just going up and down asking for donations for charity. I do that at this time of year. I made that big trip last night delivering the presents to all the little kiddies all over the world, so they could wake up to their stockings."

Detective Crowley frowned at the man. "This isn't the time for jokes."

"No, it's not. I wouldn't joke about a thing like that."

Ettie asked, "What do you think happened to

him, Ronald?"

Detective Crowley pointed at the man's neck. "Looks like he's been strangled with something." He looked around on the snowy ground. "Whatever they strangled him with, they could've taken it with them unless it's already been covered by snow. "There are no drag marks so it looks like he didn't go any closer to your house than this."

Ettie looked to where Crowley was pointing.

Crowley breathed out heavily. He looked Santa Claus up and down. "The police will need you to make a statement. Ettie, can you take this man inside? All of you stay in the house and I'll wait here by the body."

"Yes, come into the house," Ettie said to Santa. "I've got some warm food and drink to keep out the cold."

Once they got inside, Ettie suggested to Myra that she take a blanket outside for Crowley to cover himself with. Ettie then wasted no time hurrying to the kitchen to tell Elsa-May that Earl Fuller had been found murdered in their front yard.

"Strangled! That's what Detective Crowley said."

"Ettie, did you say Earl Fuller?"

"*Jah,* that's the one. Myra said she was going to call and tell him not to come. She knew him, but they'd had a falling out. Earl's abandoned wife is here, and Moses."

Elsa-May added, "And you remember that Earl ran away with Moses' daughter, don't you?"

"*Jah,* we talked about this earlier." Ettie rubbed her chin.

"I've got chills running up and down me, Ettie." Elsa-May pulled out a kitchen chair and sat down.

Naomi Fuller came into the kitchen just as the sisters had finished talking. "Can I help with anything in here?"

"Sit down, Naomi," Elsa-May said matter-of-factly.

Ettie continued, "*Jah,* I'm afraid we have some bad news for you."

After they had told Naomi that her husband, Earl, who'd run out on her years ago, was now lying dead in the front yard, she stared into space.

"Are you sure that it's him?" she eventually asked.

Ettie nodded. "He has quite distinctive features."

"Well, it serves him right. I suppose you think it's dreadful of me to say such a thing, but he ruined my life when he ran off. I was never permitted to marry again because the bishop thought there was a chance he would return. Now I'm free to marry, but it's too late for me." She pulled a tissue out of her sleeve and wiped her nose.

Elsa-May patted her on her shoulder.

"Excuse me. I need to go to the bathroom."

When Naomi was gone, Elsa-May said, "We need to get all these people fed."

"Okay. Everybody can take a plate and help themselves buffet-style."

"There would be no other way to do it."

Ten minutes later, people filed into the kitchen to get their Christmas meal. All except Santa, who was still warming himself by the fire.

Ettie walked over to him. "Would you like

something to eat? Or maybe a hot drink perhaps to warm you up?"

"Mrs. Claus won't be too happy if I eat before I get home."

"And how are you going to get home? Did you drive here? There's a phone in the shanty down the road if you'd like to call a taxi."

"I don't need a car or a taxi. I've got the reindeer and the sled. They're coming to get me later."

"How about a hot drink, then? A cup of hot tea?"

"You're very kind, Ettie."

Ettie giggled. "You know my name."

"I know everyone's name. It's my job to watch all the little children to see if they've been naughty or nice."

Ettie knew he'd had to have heard Crowley or someone else call her by name. She leaned in toward him. "I'll go and get you a cup of tea, but before I do, I'll need to warn you about Detective Kelly. He'll be here shortly and he won't take kindly to you if you keep up your Santa Claus act. He has no sense of humour." Ettie shook her head.

"None at all! Unless he's the one making the joke. That's the only thing he finds funny." Ettie stared at the man hoping he'd take her advice.

When the man just stared back at her without a word, Ettie gave him a couple of comforting pats on his shoulder and then left to fetch his hot tea.

Chapter 4

Ettie had told Crowley about all the people in their house who knew Earl—people who would be pleased that the man was now dead. She listened while Crowley relayed the information by phone to Detective Kelly who was on his way there.

After Ettie gave the man in the Santa suit some hot tea, she turned around to face Moses Stoll.

"Is it true, Ettie?"

"*Jah,* it's Earl Fuller and he's dead."

"How's Naomi taking it?" he asked.

"She's upset."

Moses rubbed his beard. "What was he doing here in your street, Ettie? You wouldn't have invited him here, would you?"

"He wasn't in my street, he was in my yard. It looked like he was coming to the house. But no, I didn't invite him."

"It seems a strange thing for him to turn up

around these parts after all this time."

"You remember my *dochder,* Myra, don't you?"

"*Jah,* I do. I was speaking to her earlier in the evening."

"She had been having complications with Earl in regard to some business matters. She hasn't quite said what yet, but she said she invited him here to make amends. She had no idea that I was having so many people here tonight. Neither did she ask me if he'd be welcome in my *haus.*"

Frozen-looking Detective Crowley hurried inside the front door and crossed over to the fire with his hands outstretched.

"Are the police here now?" Ettie asked.

"Yes they've just arrived, along with Kelly. They're gathering a team of forensics as quickly as they can." He shook his head. "This was often my busiest time of year when I was on the force. Domestic disputes and suicides are rife at this time of year."

Ettie gasped. "That's dreadful."

"It's reality."

After Ettie walked back to the front door, she peeped out to see that the place was lit up with police car headlights and portable floodlights. Blue and red lights on top of the cars were flashing illuminating the front garden.

It was then that Ettie saw that an officer was pulling a man out of a nearby car. She squinted to see if she could see who it was. Myra came up next to her and looked out the door.

"That's my friend I told you about. Michael." Myra stepped outside and hurried over.

Ettie hurried after Myra to see what she could find out. She and Myra arrived just as Detective Kelly had approached the car and was questioning Michael about why he was there.

The man ignored the detective and looked over at Myra. "Hello, I changed my mind about coming."

"According to one of my officers, you were trying to drive away," Kelly said gruffly.

Michael turned his attention back to Detective Kelly. "It seems the car battery's gone dead. I pulled up here and sat for some time wondering if I should go in. I stopped the engine, and when I tried to start it nothing happened. I'll need to call the auto club."

"Not right now, you won't. We'll need to ask you some questions." Kelly nodded to the car that the police were now searching behind him. "Was this car here when you pulled up?"

"I don't remember. I think so. Yes, I think it was."

Detective Kelly glanced at Ettie. "Crowley tells me the deceased man's name was Earl Fuller."

Michael gasped and leaned on his car. "He's dead? Is that what all this is about? I didn't know why all these cars were here."

Kelly looked back at him. "That's right. There's been a murder."

Myra said, "Detective, we both know Earl, Michael and I. Or that is, we knew the man. Michael didn't have anything to do with his murder and neither did I. My mother invited me to her Christmas party and said she wanted to make amends. Michael and I would like to leave."

Ettie raised her eyebrows, wondering if it was a good time to tell Myra she didn't send her an invitation.

Detective Kelly said, "No one is going anywhere. No one is leaving your house, Ettie." Kelly called out, "Ronson!"

A handsome young man in a suit ran up to Kelly. "Yes, sir?"

"Don't let anybody leave, and take down everyone's names and addresses. Don't leave anyone out. Understand?"

"Right, sir. Yes, sir." The young man headed toward Ettie's house.

Ronson was handsome, with short dark hair and a pleasant manner—a man any mother would've been proud of. Ettie assumed he must've been a newly appointed detective.

Kelly turned his attention to Ettie. "I'm sorry about this, Mrs. Smith, but we're going to need to borrow your house for a while. The snow's heavily drifted on the road leading to the station."

Ettie's fingertips flew to her mouth. "For how

long?"

"For however long it takes."

Myra's boyfriend put his hand on her shoulder and guided her back to the house, and Ettie was left alone with Kelly.

"Before you start to question everybody, there's something I must tell you," Ettie said to Kelly.

"That doesn't surprise me in the least." He said shaking his head. After he'd pulled a sour face, his voice lilted upward in a sing-song manner. "Yes?"

"You see, the thing is, neither Elsa-May or I invited any of these people here. I haven't seen Myra in years. We never really saw eye-to-eye. Then tonight she was the first one to knock on our door. Then, one after the other, everyone came to the house. Most of them aren't people that my sister and I are particularly friendly with. You see, two of my guests in the house have been dreadfully wronged by Earl Fuller."

The detective lowered his head while still holding Ettie's gaze. "Could it be possible that you invited these people yourself and then forgot?"

Ettie shook her head vigorously. "No, no! Neither of us invited them. Everyone received an invitation from us and the invitation apparently said to bring food. Everyone has turned up with food. Elsa-May and I would never ask our guests to bring anything with them."

Ettie then narrowed her eyes at the detective when she realized that he had made a negative remark about her age. She was sure he wouldn't have said such a thing to a younger person. "We're hardly losing our minds, Detective. Our bodies might be old but our minds are still good."

"Forgive me I didn't mean to offend, I'm just trying to make sense of everything."

"Neither of us invited anyone here tonight, and don't you think it's strange that many of the people here are enemies of Earl Fuller?"

"Tell me more?"

As he and Ettie walked toward the house, she told the detective all she knew about Earl Fuller and the people he had upset.

"Let me get this straight, Mrs. Smith. You didn't

invite anyone here, and your daughter invited Earl Fuller?"

"Yes, but only because she didn't know that Naomi, that was his wife, and Moses Stoll were both here."

"Did anybody leave the house and then return? Could anyone have slipped out of the house, killed the man, and came back inside?"

"It's hard to say because Elsa-May and I were in the kitchen at the time and we walked out just as Santa Claus burst through the door and announced that he had found a dead man."

"Santa Claus?"

"Yes, Santa Claus opened the door with a gust of snow. It was quite dramatic and then he called out that he found a dead man."

"Santa Claus?"

"Yes, Santa Claus. A man dressed as him, of course. I know it's not the real Santa. I mean, I don't believe there is a real one."

"And is the man who dressed up as Santa Claus… I'm hoping he's still inside your house?"

"Yes, yes."

"Good. I was hoping he wasn't an apparition."

"I'll introduce you to him."

"I'll start with him. Mrs. Smith, I'm going to need to take over your kitchen."

"Fine. Do whatever you have to do."

Detective Kelly walked into the house, leaving a team of people in the street photographing, measuring, and raking through the snow, collecting evidence.

Ettie and Elsa-May moved all the food into the living room so people could keep on eating.

Kelly asked Crowley if he would assist with the questioning while the young detective, Ronson took notes and made the recordings.

Ettie stayed by the door of the kitchen so she could listen. They called in Santa first.

"Can I have your name for the record?" Kelly asked the man in the red suit.

"Santa Claus."

Kelly snarled, "We need your real name."

"Santa Claus."

"This is a murder investigation. Apparently you found the body, which makes you suspect number one. If I were you, I'd drop the act and cooperate fully."

"I *am* telling you my real name."

Kelly breathed out heavily and gave a sideways look at Ronson who had pen poised, ready to take notes.

Kelly continued, "Address?"

"Santa's workshop, the North Pole."

Ettie peeped around the kitchen door, worried for the man. She had warned him Kelly wouldn't find this funny.

"I'll give you one more chance and then I'll take you down to the station and put you in lock-up. State your full name and address for the record."

"Santa Claus. Santa's Workshop, the North Pole."

Detective Kelly leaned forward.

"Have you been drinking?"

"Yes! Last night I had a few. Sometimes the kiddies leave me a beer and a slice of Christmas cake. Some leave carrots for the reindeers. It would be rude if I didn't drink what they left out for me." He patted his large stomach and gave a chuckle.

Detective Kelly turned to Ronson. "Have someone take him back to the station and then come straight back here."

"No! You must believe I am the real Santa. My beard's real. You can pull it if you want." Santa tugged at his white beard and offered it for them to pull.

Ronson reached out his hand and then looked at Kelly. "Can I?"

Kelly pinched his eyebrows together, remained tight-lipped and shook his head.

Ronson immediately withdrew his hand.

"Have Phillips take him and put him in lock him up for the night. He can sleep off his drunkenness. You come straight back here. Understand?"

"Yes, sir." Ronson bounded to his feet. "What about the snowdrifts on the way to the station, sir?"

Kelly frowned at the young man. "They'll have to wait in the car until someone clears the snow, or it melts!"

"Yes, sir." Ronson looked at Santa. "This way."

Together, Ronson and Santa walked out of the house.

Kelly said, "Crowley, did that man say anything to you about how he found the body?"

"He said he didn't touch anything. Except he leaned down to touch his neck to feel for a pulse and there was nothing. It was then that he ran into the house."

"Did he see anyone about?"

"He saw no one else in the street. He mumbled something about someone in the car across the road."

"I doubt we can believe anything he said. He could've murdered the man. We'll need to run his prints."

Chapter 5

The next person to be interviewed was Myra, and Ettie sat in the kitchen with her. Ettie and her daughter were on one side of the table, with Detective Kelly on the other, beside Crowley, the retired detective. Ronson came back inside from delivering Santa to one of the officers outside and he sat back down beside Kelly.

Ronson then informed Myra he'd be recording the conversation and taking notes. After Myra gave her full name and address for the record, the questioning began.

Detective Kelly began, "Myra, how did you know the deceased?"

"I knew him when I was in the community. As you have probably already guessed, I was raised Amish." She shot a sideways glare at her mother displaying her disapproval. "I went to the same school as Earl and saw him often after that—Sunday meetings, community events and the like. We were never close back then. I left the community when I became old enough. I ran into Earl a little over a year ago."

"And you were the one who invited him here?"

"I did, because I thought I should try and bury the hatchet and make a fresh start with people in my life. That was to be my new year's resolution—to get along with people. Things were fine at first between Earl and I, then we got on each other's nerves. I thought if my mother can say she's sorry then I can find it in my heart to make peace with someone too."

"Where did you run into him again?" Kelly asked. "You knew him in the Amish community, and then when did you meet him again?"

"We met again on a motivational cruise."

Detective Kelly placed his elbows on the table and rested his chin on his knuckles. "Could you describe to me exactly what a motivational cruise is?"

"It's a normal kind of cruise, but the price of the ticket included a round of lectures by Ralph

Bounty, as well. Have you heard of him?"

Kelly pulled a face turning his lips downward at the corners. "Can't say that I have."

"I've been reading his books for years. He's a motivational speaker and he also gives one-on-one business advice. He helped me develop an idea I've had for some time. It was on that cruise, at one of Ralph's lectures, that I saw Earl. It was the first time I'd seen him since I left the community."

"Go on."

"We sat next to each other because neither of us knew anyone else there. I told him about my business plans and he said he had some people he knew who might like to invest in the concept. He asked me all about it and I had no reason not to tell him. He even sat in on my private sessions with Ralph."

"How did you two have a falling out?" Crowley asked.

"I'm getting to that. When we got back, I found out that he lived close by. He seemed to turn up everywhere I went. I finally had to tell him I was no longer interested in his investors. The man was beginning to disturb me."

"How did he take that?" Kelly asked.

"He kept away for a while, but when I was about to sign a lease for a building for my wellness center, I found out he was doing the very same thing close by. The realtor mentioned that it was odd that someone else was looking for space for a wellness center and she let his name slip. He had more money to throw at it than I. There was nothing I could do so I had to shelve my idea. If I'd gone ahead, my business would never have lasted. Not with a larger competitor nearby."

"Did you go ahead elsewhere?" Ronson asked. "Or did Earl end up going ahead?"

Kelly turned and stared at Ronson, who lowered his head. Kelly then turned back to Myra. "Did he go ahead with his plans, Myra?"

"He wouldn't have had time to do so. This all happened recently."

"So what you're saying is it's convenient for you that this man is now dead?"

"Yes, I suppose it is, if you look at it like that."

"And the man we picked up in the car with the dead battery, he's a business acquaintance of yours?" Kelly asked.

"No, he's my…" her eyes flickered to Ronald Crowley. "He is sort of like my boyfriend."

Detective Kelly frowned. "Sort of? Define that for me."

"We live together."

Ettie was shocked and she could see by Ronald's face that he was disappointed.

Kelly's face remained solemn. "And for how long have you two been cohabiting?"

"Around a year. No wait, I think it's about eighteen months now."

"When did you last see Earl Fuller alive?"

"We had a big argument when we bumped into each other at a restaurant about a week ago."

"What happened?"

"He was out having dinner with some people and so was I. We saw each other and one thing led to another. I asked him why he was copying my idea.

He ended up yelling accusations at me and then we were asked to leave the restaurant. He somehow twisted things in his mind to believe that it was his idea. That's the only way I could make sense of his actions."

"And was your live-in-boyfriend with you at that time?"

"Yes, Michael was there."

Kelly leaned forward. "Maria, how did you happen to be here tonight?"

"It's Myra, not Maria."

"Oh, I'm sorry. I don't know why I have difficulty with that name."

"That's okay. I often get that. My mother sent me an invitation saying she would like me to come so we can sort out our differences. She said she'd like us to have a Christmas that we'd never forget. Those were her very words."

"Myra, I never sent you an invitation."

Myra stared at her mother. "Yes, you did. Otherwise, I wouldn't be here."

Ettie shook her head. "I never sent you anything."

"Are you sure?"

"Quite sure. And neither did I send anyone an invitation. People just started coming here. At first, I was angry with Elsa-May because I thought she had invited everyone without telling me. I was quite annoyed because our house is so small." Ettie turned to Detective Kelly and explained. "The house is far too small for this number of people. I'd never invite this many people and neither would my sister."

"So you don't want to say you're sorry?" Myra asked her mother.

"What would I be sorry for?"

Myra's mouth fell open. "You don't know?"

"No, I don't."

"For raising me in the Amish community and keeping me away from normal society—the real world."

"You should be thanking me for that."

Myra shook her head. "I knew it was too good to be true."

Crowley cleared his throat. "Myra, do you still

have that invitation?"

"Yes, I do. I've got it in my handbag in the living room."

"Mind if we take a look?"

"Do you want me to get it right now?"

"Yes, please."

Myra pushed out her chair and left the kitchen.

Detective Kelly said to Ettie, "Who do you think would've played this prank on you and your sister?"

Ettie thought for a moment. "I don't know anyone who would've done it. I'm not particularly close with Naomi or Moses, so I was surprised at them showing up at my door, but it makes sense now because they both had grievances with Earl."

Ronson said, "So you think this was all a set up to kill Earl? Perhaps to give someone an alibi, or to cover someone's tracks in some way?"

Detective Kelly glared at Ronson. "Just take the notes."

"Yes, sir. Sorry, sir." Ronson hung his head and looked back down at his notes.

“He’s new,” Kelly explained to Ettie.

“That’s quite all right. We all have to start somewhere.”

The young man looked up at Ettie and offered a weak smile.

Myra flounced back into the room with the invitation and passed it over to Detective Kelly who scanned his eyes up and down it.

“Can I see it?” Ettie asked.

Kelly handed it to Ettie. “It’s nothing like my handwriting.”

“It looked like it to me,” Myra said.

Kelly leaned over and plucked the invitation out of Ettie’s hands.

“We might have to hang onto this, Marie, if that’s okay.”

“It’s Myra! Keep it! I don’t want it.” As she sat, she gave her mother a sour look and then looked back at Kelly. “Do you have any more questions, Detective?”

“Not for now, but we might need to speak to you later.”

"Later, another day? Can Michael and I go home now?"

"No!" Crowley said before Kelly had a chance. "We'll need to speak to everybody before anyone leaves; that means Michael too."

"What happened to Santa?" Myra asked.

"Santa Claus left," Kelly said bluntly.

"We had to take him down to the station to lock him up. We think he'd been drinking," Ronson explained.

"You're locking up Santa Claus on Christmas day?"

"He's not the real Santa," Ronson said.

Detective Kelly said, "That's all for now, thank you Mara."

"It's Myra," she corrected him once again.

"Sorry. Thank you, Myra."

When Myra left the kitchen, Kelly turned to Ronson. "Why are you going on about the real Santa? I suppose you believe that there is a real one living at the North Pole?" Kelly laughed and looked at Crowley, expecting him to laugh too.

Crowley gave a slight raise of his eyebrows and remained silent.

"I didn't want people to think poorly of the police for locking up an old man at Christmas time. And it does look bad to have Santa in a cell at Christmas time."

Kelly frowned. "It's for his own good. And for the good of the investigation." Kelly's phone sounded and he pulled it out of his inner coat pocket. "Yes? Well, that explains a lot. Keep him there and I'll talk to him again when I get there." Kelly put the phone back in his pocket.

"Is everything all right?" Ettie asked.

"We had a report of a missing person from one of the mental health facilities. One of their patients went missing in his Santa suit. Their patient believes he's Santa." Kelly chuckled as he explained. "He goes missing every Christmas, delivering presents and trying to get back to his wife at the North Pole."

"That's sad," Ettie said. "Poor Santa."

"Does he have a history of violence?" Crowley asked.

"They said he's harmless." Kelly's attention turned to Ettie. "Mrs. Smith, would you mind bringing Michael in to us?"

"Yes, of course I'll get him."

"And then can you wait in the living room?"

When Ettie told Michael the police wanted to talk with him, she showed him to the kitchen and waited outside so she could hear everything. She knew it wasn't good to eavesdrop, but a man had been murdered outside her house, so she figured that gave her the right.

Detective Kelly wasted no time getting to the point. "Michael Skully, did you kill Earl Fuller?"

"No! I did not."

"Why were you in the street at the same time the man was murdered?"

"Myra asked me to come here and at first I said no, but then I changed my mind. I thought Myra and her mother would've had enough time to reconcile and I wanted to meet Myra's mother."

"Did you see anyone else in the street?"

"No. I stopped the car, and in my mind I went

back and forth about whether I should go inside, and I decided it was a bad idea so I tried to start the car to drive away, but it wouldn't start. Next thing I know, the place was swarming with cops."

"Did you know the deceased?"

"I met him once or twice."

"That's a yes?" Ronson asked.

"Yes."

Kelly continued, "And you knew he was an enemy of your… girlfriend's?"

"I knew he'd stolen her idea. Myra and I do talk about things."

Ettie peeped around the door to see Kelly lower his right eyebrow the way he did when someone was annoying him. Michael's tone was bordering on sarcastic.

Kelly looked over and saw Ettie. "Mrs. Smith, kindly close the door, would you?"

Ettie closed the door, annoyed with herself for not staying out of sight.

The next person to be interviewed was Moses who in his own quiet way made it clear that he wasn't happy with Earl for taking his daughter away. He hadn't seen his daughter since that day and didn't even know where she was. They asked him about the Christmas invitation that had been sent to him. Moses was able to tell them word-for-word what the invitation had said. Ettie heard the words through the door. 'A Christmas dinner that you'll never forget.'

It was certainly a Christmas day that Ettie wouldn't easily forget.

The next person to sit in front of the detective was Naomi Fuller. Naomi was Earl's wife whom he'd deserted. Naomi was understandably hurt and angry with Earl for leaving her to run away with another woman.

Ettie couldn't blame Naomi for the bitterness she still carried. With the Amish there was no divorce and Naomi had been reasonably young when he'd left her. She was forced to live a lonely life without children or husband.

As all the other guests filed into the kitchen one by one for their questioning, Ettie realized that all of them were people Myra knew from her childhood. This was all to do with Myra. Everyone had come there tonight because of Myra.

Ettie had managed to hear enough through the closed door to learn that no one had noticed anyone go outside her house and then return.

Elsa-May came up beside Ettie. "Have they finished interviewing everyone yet?"

"There are only a couple more people to go now. And then there's you."

"Well, I know nothing."

"Elsa-May, I never thought I'd hear you say those words."

Elsa-May chuckled.

Ettie added, "And they found out that Santa Claus wasn't really Santa Claus."

"Thanks for enlightening me."

"Well, *he* didn't know that. He thinks he's the real Santa Claus who lives at the North Pole, when he really lives in some kind of an institution."

"He thinks he's really Santa Claus?" Elsa-May asked.

"It seems so."

Chapter 6

After the detective finished interviewing everyone, Kelly took Ronson's notes and was going over them when Ettie stepped into the kitchen.

"Mind if I have a word?"

"Take a seat."

Ettie sat down in front of the three men. "I don't think it's a prank that people were invited here tonight. With the exception of Michael, everyone here is someone that Myra knew from when she was growing up in the community."

"So it's all about Myra?" Detective Kelly asked.

"I'm sure of it."

"Do you have any idea why Earl would come to your house?" Kelly asked.

Before she could answer, Crowley asked, "Do you think he also had an invitation?"

"Myra said she invited him here."

Kelly took his phone from his pocket. "Let me

make a call. I'll see if they found anything in his car." A few minutes later, Kelly ended the call not looking too happy. "He had an invitation in his car from Myra saying to meet him at this address. The note was signed from Myra and said she hoped they could sort out their differences once and for all."

Ettie's jaw dropped open when it dawned on her that things now didn't look good for Myra.

"Ettie, can you send Myra in again?" Kelly asked.

Ettie hurried to fetch Myra who was sitting close to Michael on the couch.

"The detective wants to speak to you again."

"Okay." Myra followed Ettie back into the kitchen.

Once Myra and Ettie were seated, Kelly told her about the note found in Earl's car.

"Yes, I sent it. I wanted to make amends with him."

"But you've got no idea who sent the invitations on behalf of your mother and your aunt?"

"Do you think I killed Earl? It couldn't have been me because I didn't even leave the house."

"It appears no one did," Kelly said.

"Or, no one noticed anyone leave the house," Ronson added.

Kelly ignored Ronson. "I understand your concerns, Mrs. Smith, about what happened here tonight, but I think what we might have here is nothing more than a prank. Earl's murder could have been a random killing. The prankster who sent those invitations is probably under your roof right now. Maybe it's someone who knew Myra back in the day, and knew of her annoyance with Earl. They could very well have wanted to watch some drama play out before them. People are strange like that."

"But why was he murdered?" Ettie said.

"I'd say if someone was deluded enough to believe they are really Santa Claus they would probably be mad enough to kill someone."

"He seemed a harmless old man." Ettie said. "Are you thinking he murdered Earl?"

"It's possible. We've got everyone's handwriting." He turned to Ronson. "Haven't we?"

"Yes, sir, and everyone's names and addresses."

"We'll run the handwriting up to an analyst and I'm hundred percent positive that we'll find a match from someone here tonight."

Ettie nodded. "I'd feel better knowing who organized this whole thing."

"What happens now?" Myra asked.

"We'll see what the forensics team has found, and meanwhile Earl's relatives will need to be informed."

Ettie said, "There's Naomi his wife, whom you've already spoken with, and then there are a few brothers scattered around the country. I'm sure Naomi could inform them."

Myra added, "He didn't have any close family."

"Can people go now?" Ettie asked.

Detective Kelly looked at Ronson. "Have we got everything we need?"

"Yes, sir."

"Good." He looked back at Ettie. "I'll just make

a call to see where the evidence technicians are up to." Kelly made the call and then slipped his phone back in his pocket. "The body's been taken away and his car towed." He stared at Ettie. "Oh, I'm sorry, Mrs. Smith. I know you don't like anyone using phones in your house."

"Under the circumstances, that's quite all right."

He glanced at his watch. "Two o'clock already. I'm sorry it's been such a long night."

"Oh, it's past midnight?" Ettie asked, worried about Snowy closed in Elsa-May's bedroom for so long.

"Sorry to keep you up so late, Mrs Smith. And it's a pity all this has ruined your Christmas day."

"That's okay. Today is Second Christmas."

"You have a Second Christmas?"

"That's right. Some Amish communities celebrate a Second Christmas on the twenty-sixth of December."

"I had no idea."

Crowley chuckled. "It surprised me when I heard about it, too. It seemed quite odd. No offence or anything, Ettie."

"None taken."

Detective Kelly walked into the living room and told the guests they could go home.

"Do you know who did it yet?" Moses asked as he stood up from one of the chairs near the fire.

"Not at this stage," Kelly answered. "The investigation's ongoing. You'll all most likely be contacted again if we need to ask you any more questions."

One by one, people left, much like they'd arrived.

"Well, Mother, it was good to see you again."

"I do hope we can work out our differences one day," Ettie said.

"I doubt it," Myra said as her eyes darted to Crowley, who was staring at her. "And it was good to see you too, Ronald."

"Come on, Myra," Michael said, taking hold of her arm.

When Myra and Michael walked out the front door, Crowley stood staring after them.

Ettie felt sorry for him. He clearly had feelings

for Myra.

"I'll stay until everyone goes," Crowley said as he turned his gaze toward Ettie.

"Thank you."

Ettie and Elsa-May were finally able to go to bed an hour later.

Ettie lay in bed thinking about what had happened that day. Detective Kelly had promised them he'd keep in contact and let them know what the investigators found out.

It was awful to think that they were inside enjoying Christmas when a man was outside taking his last breath. And, why, and how, was Myra involved in it all?

Chapter 7

Ettie woke the next morning, pulled on her dressing gown and headed into the kitchen. She sighed heavily when she saw plates and dishes all over the place. She'd been too tired to notice the state the kitchen had been in the night before. They had never before left the place in a mess like this.

Elsa-May came up behind her and stared at the pile of dirty plates and bowls.

"Merry Christmas to us," Ettie said.

Elsa-May chortled. "Come on, it won't take long for the both of us to get this sorted."

Just as they had washed and dried the last plate, three loud knocks sounded at the door.

"What now?" Ettie asked. "I hope this all doesn't play out again for Second Christmas. If it does, I'm not letting anyone inside."

Elsa-May said, "I'll try to work out who these serving dishes belong to while you answer the door."

Ettie sighed figuring that once again, Elsa-May had taken the easier option. "I hope it's not Santa Claus asking directions to the North Pole." Ettie opened the door to see Myra. She looked around for her boyfriend, but she'd come alone.

"Can I come in, Mother, or are you going to leave me outside all day?"

Ettie stepped aside. "Of course, you can come in."

"I couldn't sleep all night. I was too worried about what happened here yesterday." Myra sat herself heavily on the couch. "I'm worried that someone is trying to frame me for murder."

"And who do you think might be doing that?"

"You could at least tell me that no one would do that. Or, at the very least, that I was letting my imagination run away with me."

Ettie pursed her lips and was glad when Elsa-May joined them.

"Myra, did you come to get one of your serving dishes?"

"No. I came to see who might be trying to make

it look like I killed Earl."

"Oh! Who do you think it would be?"

Myra scowled. "You two are very much alike."

Ettie and Elsa-May stared at each other.

"I don't think we're anything alike," Ettie said.

"Neither do I," Elsa-May added.

"The reason I'm here is I want you both to help me figure this out. I'll drive you to my home and then I'll tell you the full story. I'll tell you everything about Earl and myself, and hopefully we'll be able to find out what happened."

"What makes you think we'll be able to do that?" Elsa-May asked.

"You helped me when that no good husband of mine disappeared a few years ago. So I thought you'd be able to help me now." She stood up. "Unless you don't want to."

Ettie pushed herself to her feet. "We do want to help you, don't we, Elsa-May?"

Elsa-May nodded. "We'll help you as much as we can, Myra."

Myra looked round the house. "I don't feel

comfortable in this Amish setting with the bland walls in this dark little dingy house. I know you've tried to brighten it up with the Christmas lanterns and the candles, but it's still depressing."

Ettie looked around at the place she called home. It was small, but it wasn't dark. For Christmas they had white candles in the windowsills and had hung lanterns from the ceilings to give the place the feel of Christmas.

"Where would you rather talk?" Elsa-May asked

"As I said, I'd like to take the two of you back to my house."

"You live close by?" Ettie asked.

Myra stared at her mother. "You really *didn't* send the invitation. You didn't even have my new address."

Ettie nodded. "That's what I've said all along."

"I live around half an hour away."

"Can we bring Snowy?" Elsa-May asked, looking at her dog curled up on his bed in the corner.

"Is he house trained?" Myra asked.

"Yes, he is."

"More or less," Ettie added.

"He is, Ettie."

"Okay," Myra answered, "But you'll have to put him on your lap in the car. I don't want him on my good leather seats."

As they set off, Ettie asked Myra if she would mind stopping by at Jeremiah and Ava's house. Ettie was keen to explain to Ava why they hadn't stopped by the night before.

Myra reluctantly agreed and told Ettie to be quick. Once they were there, Ettie got out of the car. "Are you coming, Elsa-May?"

"No. I'll stay here with Snowy."

"What about you, Myra. Do you want to come in and say hello to Ava?"

"No! I don't want to see anyone from the community even if we are related by marriage. I had my fill of Amish people last night, thank you very much."

Ettie walked to the house and knocked on the door and Ava opened it.

"Ettie!" She looked over at the car.

"I have a long story to tell you, but right now I just wanted to say I'm sorry that we didn't end up coming last. Elsa-May and I are going over to Myra's house for a few hours. She wants to talk something over with us."

"Your daughter, Myra? The one you haven't seen in years?"

"That's the one."

Ava squinted. "How did that come about?"

"Do you remember a man who used to be in the community—his name was Earl Fuller and he ran away with Moses Stoll's *dochder?"*

"Nee, I don't remember the name."

"But you know Naomi Fuller?"

"Jah."

Myra's car horn sounded.

"Oh dear. I've got a lot to tell you, but I'll have to tell you another time. In short, Earl was found murdered outside our house last night."

"Ettie, that's dreadful! I definitely want to hear the whole story."

"Tell Jeremiah we're sorry we didn't come here last night."

"Of course I'll tell him, but don't you worry about that, Ettie. Thanks for stopping by."

"We'll talk later." Ettie walked back to the car.

"What took you so long, Mother?"

"I had to tell her briefly what happened so she wouldn't hear it from anyone else first."

"I didn't drive you there to have a gossip session."

"I wasn't gossiping," Ettie said, staring at her daughter.

Chapter 8

There wasn't much talking done in the car. Myra had her face set like flint as she concentrated on the cold wet roads.

Around twenty minutes later, she turned into a suburban estate. After a few turns, she drove into a driveway and the garage door opened.

"Is this your house?" Ettie asked staring up at the two-story house in wonder. If this was Myra's home, she'd certainly come into a lot of money somewhere.

"No, Mother, I'm driving into someone else's garage. Of course this is my house."

When they got out of the car, Snowy got away from Elsa-May. Myra managed to grab him and then she placed him in Elsa-May's arms.

"You can put him out in the backyard. It's fully enclosed and part of it's covered."

"Okay."

While Elsa-May and Myra were busy putting the

dog in the backyard, Ettie wandered through the house. The door from the garage led into a grand hallway complete with hanging crystal chandelier and a sweeping staircase to one side. Ettie stared up at the high ceilings while under her feet were marble floors. As she followed the voices, she was led into a living room that opened onto a terrace. The grass outside was covered with a fine layer of snow. To her right, Ettie noticed a massive kitchen the size of what one would find in a restaurant.

"Sit, Mother," Myra called out from the yard where she stood with Elsa-May.

Ettie sank into one of the plush couches and waited until Myra returned.

Once Snowy had relieved himself, Myra allowed him back into the house, but insisted he stay on Elsa-May's lap.

"Where's Michael?" Ettie asked once Myra and Elsa-May were seated. "Doesn't he live with you?"

"He's busy. He travels a lot."

"Even over Christmas? Doesn't everything stop for the *Englishers* at this time of year?"

"Sometimes," was all that Myra said on the matter. "I wanted you both to come here so I could talk to you about what a crook Earl Fuller was. He masqueraded as my friend when all the time he was nothing but a thief. He stole my business ideas."

Ettie wondered if she would tell her more than she told the detectives, otherwise what was the point of her being there? She'd heard all this before. "I told Elsa-May already what you told the detectives."

"There's more. I was ready to forgive and forget but the more I think about what he did the angrier I get. He told me he could get me investors, but I don't think he had any investors at all. I think he was somehow trying to take my money."

"How could he have leased space for his wellness center with no money?" Elsa-May asked.

"He never went ahead with it. I think he was trying to lease a bigger, better space than mine, thinking he was leaving me no choice but to finally join with him."

"It seems far fetched," Ettie said.

Snowy jumped off Elsa-May's lap.

"Get the dog," Myra yelled.

Elsa-May reached over and pulled him back and then placed him back on her lap. "Stay," she told him.

The command sounded impressive, but Snowy was not trained as well as Elsa-May liked to think.

"Don't let him get on the furniture," Myra told Elsa-May.

"I won't."

"So he was trying to encourage you to invest money into his business?" Ettie asked.

"That's right. I never felt good about it and I talked it over with Michael. Michael was the one who said I should go it alone."

"Michael encouraged you to cut Earl out?"

"Yes."

"So the first time you saw Earl away from the community was on the cruise?"

"Yes, that's right. I hadn't seen him since I left the Amish and there he was on the cruise."

"But you two were still friends after the cruise?"

Elsa-May asked.

"Yes, that's right, but then he got a little creepy. He was following me. So I told him I didn't want to be in business with him. Together we'd worked on a business plan right down to the minutest of details. Then I found out that he had jumped the gun on me and was about to use my plans in a much grander way, given the space he was looking to lease."

"You worked on the business plan together?"

"They were mostly my ideas. I'd worked them out on the cruise, with Ralph. I found out from the realtor what name the business was going to have. It seemed he told her a great deal of things. He had intended to steal my name and everything."

"How would he have had the money to do it without your investment?"

"That's a good question, Elsa-May."

Elsa-May continued, "If he was asking for your investment in his current business, it sounds like he wouldn't have had the money to go ahead with the new business. Unless he'd had investors like he'd said."

"I don't think he did. That's just it. He was holding me to ransom. He wanted me to borrow half a million dollars and we would be forty-sixty business partners. He wanted sixty percent because he said he could get the investors, but I was the one who'd come up with the concept originally."

"And was Michael putting any money into it?"

"Michael is the numbers man. I got him to look into it and he asked Earl questions and it turns out that Earl hadn't intended to put any money into it. Essentially he was trying to steal sixty percent of my business. When I said that to him, he said it was his idea and then he threatened to sue me."

"You didn't tell the police that."

"With everything I've been through I just couldn't go through the stress of it."

"So did he open the business, or where are things sitting with that?" Ettie asked while patting her daughter on her arm.

"I got a letter from his lawyer demanding I stop everything."

"Can the town take two of these wellness centers?" Elsa-May asked.

"That's just it. Probably not, but now that he's dead I don't have that problem. I can go ahead."

"Exactly what is a wellness center, Myra?" Ettie asked.

"It would be hard for you two to understand. It will have yoga classes, spiritual healing, aura cleansing, chakra healing, and other things that you wouldn't understand about."

"There's money in that kind of thing?" Ettie asked.

"People spend billions of dollars on wellness a year."

"I guess everyone is looking for something," Elsa-May said.

"And who do you think killed Earl?" Ettie asked her daughter.

"I don't know."

"Who would've benefited from having him out of the way? Besides yourself, of course."

"That's just it. That's what I'm worried about.

I don't think anyone would get more out of him being dead than what I'd gain." Myra nibbled on a fingernail before she continued, "He didn't have any friends and he wasn't in touch with his family that I know of. He was still married to Naomi, I found out last night. I'm worried that someone is trying to frame me and I'll end up in jail. I see things like that in the movies all the time."

"Surely not," Ettie said.

"Well, that's what I think. Who sent those invitations, then?"

Elsa-May said, "Detective Kelly is working on finding that out. He thinks it was someone who was at the house last night."

"What about Santa Claus? Do you think that he might have known Earl and killed him?" Myra asked.

Ettie shook her head. "He seemed to be a harmless old man who thought he was Santa Claus."

"Okay. I was too scared to say it, but now I might have to say it out loud."

Elsa-May leaned forward. "What is it, Myra?"

"I think it was Naomi who killed him."

"Why do you think that?" Ettie asked.

"He left her alone to become a shrivelled-up cranky old woman. If a woman doesn't have children in the community, she's an outcast."

Ettie shook her head. "I don't think that's right, Myra. But I do see that she'd be upset about being abandoned."

"After all these years, though?" Elsa-May asked.

Myra's eyes opened wide. "I could see the bitterness on her face. What he'd done to her was probably building up and building up over many years."

"Yes, but what does this any of this have to do with you?" Ettie asked.

Myra frowned at her mother. "Why would it have to have anything to do with me?"

Ettie continued, "Everybody who came to the house last night was someone you knew when you were growing up."

"See? I was right. Someone's trying to frame me and it could be Naomi. I never really got along with her."

You never got along with anyone, Ettie thought.

"You think Naomi killed him and then tried to make it look like you did it?" Elsa-May asked Myra.

"Yes. It seems a reasonable assumption."

"There are many easier ways to kill a man and, like Ettie said, she probably would've done it along time ago if she was ever going to do it."

Ettie pulled her mouth to one side. "I don't think that's exactly what I said."

"Well, what about Crowley?" Elsa-May asked, changing the subject. "How did you feel seeing him again?"

"I never thought we were suited."

"How did you feel seeing him again?" Elsa-May repeated.

Ettie frowned at Elsa-May being brave enough to ask Myra something so personal.

"I won't say there isn't something there between us because there is. I don't think anything will ever work out for us because I have Michael now."

"And what kind of work does Michael do?"

"He's a sales rep for a pharmaceutical company. He travels all over the place."

"And how long have you known him?" Elsa-May asked while Ettie sat in silence, anxious to hear the answers but not bold enough to ask the questions.

Myra laughed. "I didn't bring you both here to talk about my relationship."

Elsa-May laughed along with her. "We're just curious. We've never seen you so happy."

A smile brightened Myra's face. "I've known him for about eighteen months."

"But haven't you been living together for around that same amount of time?"

"That's right." Myra sighed. "But I want to tell you more about Earl. I'd applied for a grant and then I also found out that he had applied for the same one."

"A business grant for money?"

"Yes."

Elsa-May tapped a finger on her chin. "So he

was doing everything he could to have you join with him?"

"Yes."

"That was quite a compliment," Ettie said.

"Annoying was what it was."

"Was he doing it out of love? Do you think he could've been in love with you?" Elsa-May asked.

Ettie added, "You did say he didn't have anyone in his life. Perhaps he was harbouring a secret crush on you."

"I don't think so. He never said anything. Anyway, I wanted you both to know everything so you can help me to figure the whole thing out. I'm convinced that Naomi is trying to set me up for his murder. I don't know why she'd hate me so much. The person she should hate is Earl."

Elsa-May and Ettie exchanged glances.

"Mother, I know you're a friend of Crowley and that Detective Kelly. I need you to convince both of them that I had nothing to do with Earl's death."

Chapter 9

The next morning Elsa-May and Ettie had just sat down when they were disturbed by a loud knock on their front door.

"I would say that's Detective Kelly," Ettie said.

"Why would you say that?" Elsa-May asked.

"Who else would it be at this early hour?"

Elsa-May stood up. "We'll soon find out."

Ettie headed to the door behind Elsa-May. In front of them when they opened their door, stood Detective Kelly in a crumpled suit, looking like he hadn't slept for two days.

Elsa-May opened the door wider. "Detective Kelly, come in."

When he stepped through the door, Ettie asked him if he would like some breakfast.

"No thank you." He sniffed the air. "Is that pancakes I can smell?"

"Yes. There's still some batter left if you would like to change your answer and have some. It won't take a moment."

Ettie added, "It won't take any time and we can do that while you're talking."

"I'd like that very much." A smile hinted around Kelly's lips. "Thank you"

"This way," Elsa-May said as she walked back into the kitchen.

Ettie sat down at the table with Detective Kelly while Elsa-May dropped a measure of the pancake batter into the hot buttered frying pan.

"Did you find out who murdered Earl?" Ettie asked.

A chuckle caught in his throat. "No, not yet."

"Is there anything we can do to help?"

"Yes, that's why I'm here."

"Just tell us what you need," Elsa-May said.

"While some of your Amish people were helpful when they were here in your house, when I asked them to make official statements all of them declined."

"What do you need from us?" Ettie asked.

"I need to know if I should do further

investigations on Moses Stoll and Naomi Fuller. Each had a reason to hate him."

"Exactly what would you like to know from them?" Ettie asked.

"Naomi Fuller was still married to the man, is that correct?"

"Yes, they never got a divorce and I think you had that confirmed."

Elsa-May added, "Unless he filed for divorce it wouldn't have been permitted, because she wouldn't have been allowed."

"You're right, Ettie. The records show she was still his legal wife and heir to his estate."

"Detective, you make it sound like he had a substantial amount of money to leave, but my impression from Myra was that the man didn't have much money at all."

Kelly chuckled. "We searched his apartment and found bank statements and other paperwork that show a totally different side of Earl Fuller."

"Do you mean he had a lot of money?" Elsa-May asked.

"That's a very subjective question. To you and me the amount of money he had would seem quite substantial, but to somebody else it may not."

"Exactly how much money are we talking about?" Ettie asked.

"Two and a half million dollars. And we found evidence of various real estate holdings."

Ettie raised her eyebrows. She would've thought that would've been a lot of money in anybody's opinion. "Since he had so much money, I wonder why he was trying to use Myra's?"

"I suppose that's how people become rich by using other people's money."

"Myra would've never guess that he would've had that much money. I'm certain of it."

"Let's just keep this to ourselves at the moment. Anything I tell you ladies is just between us."

Ettie nodded. "Yes, of course."

"Anyway, the point is that Naomi Fuller has just become a very rich woman. Unless, of course, a later will surfaces."

Elsa-May turned around from the stove. "Well,

that wouldn't make up for what the man did to her."

"No, but it is a strong motive for murder. The money coupled with what he did to her, makes Naomi Fuller suspect number one."

"So where does this leave Moses?"

"I don't know what I think about him yet. Maybe they were in it together. Either of them could've slipped outside your house, murdered the man and got back into the house."

"But how would she have known he was going to be there?"

"Remember we found that note in his car from Myra?"

"That's right. I did forget that temporarily," Ettie said.

"So whoever killed him, must've been in contact with him to know the connection he had with Myra. And they would've known he was trying to get back into her good books," Elsa-May said.

"Correct," Kelly said.

"And you want us to talk with Naomi?"

"Yes. I'm torn whether she's capable of murder.

Just talking to her, she didn't seem to have it in her."

"We'll see what we can find out."

Elsa-May slid the pancakes onto a plate and placed it in front of Detective Kelly.

His face lit up as he sprinkled sugar, squeezed a little lemon over them and drizzled maple syrup over the top.

"That will be a good lining on your stomach today," Elsa-May said.

"Coffee?" Ettie asked.

"Always," Detective Kelly answered. "I'd leave it a day or two before you visit both Moses and Naomi. I don't want them to feel like people are hammering them to get information out of them. Things move slowly at this time of year. The courts won't be open until after New Year. If I have to arrest anyone, they'll be sitting in jail without bail until court opens again."

"I see," Ettie said.

"Another piece of good news is that we ran Santa's prints and he has no priors."

"That is good news. So he was just a homeless man who thinks he's Santa Claus?" Elsa-May asked as she sat down at the table.

"He's not homeless. He lives in an institution. They let him keep his Santa outfit and made him promise that he'd only wear it at Christmas. The poor old soul."

Ettie placed a cup of coffee in front of the detective and sat back down.

"Thank you, Ettie."

"So it might be right that Santa was just going up the street knocking on doors asking for donations?"

"Yes, and I wonder where those donation ended up?" Detective Kelly asked. "I'll let that go for now. There are more important things at stake."

"Did you have a good Christmas, Detective?"

Detective Kelly stared at Ettie. "It was like every other day of the year for me." He slurped a mouthful of coffee.

Chapter 10

Ettie and Elsa-May got dressed warmly, ready to visit Ava. When Ettie opened the door, she found herself face-to-face with Detective Kelly.

"Heading out somewhere?" he asked with a lopsided smile.

"Yes, we were just going to go to visit Ava. We feel we've been in the house for days," Elsa-May said.

Ettie added, "Well, I suppose we haven't, but it just feels that way."

"Come in out of the cold."

When they were all seated in the living room, Kelly said, "I was surprised to get a call this morning from the handwriting analyst."

"Are the results in?" Elsa-May asked.

"Yes they are and that's why I'm here. I thought I would let you know that Myra's live-in-boyfriend is responsible for sending those invitations."

Ettie gasped. "No!"

Elsa-May frowned. “I don’t believe it.”

“Do you think he killed Earl?” Ettie asked.

“It’s the strongest lead we have so far. As you said yourself, Mrs. Smith, apart from him, all the people at your house were people Myra knew from when she was growing up in your Amish community.”

Ettie felt sick to the stomach. How would poor Myra be taking this?

“He’s being picked up now and brought down to the station. I thought you should know because your daughter might be upset.” He stared at Ettie.

Ettie nodded. “Yes, she would be devastated. She would’ve had no idea. I appreciate you letting us know.”

“I just thought I should have the decency of telling you in person.”

“Yes, that was very considerate of you.”

He sniffed the air. “Can I smell coffee?”

“No, we drank tea this morning,” Elsa-May said matter-of-factly.

“It’s no trouble if you would like to make you

some coffee," Ettie said.

Detective Kelly smiled. "I'd appreciate a cup."

"I'll get it, Ettie." Elsa-May stood up. "Coming right up. And maybe a couple of sugar cookies?"

"Yes please."

"And do you know the cause of death, yet?" Ettie asked.

"The man was strangled and he also had a drug in his system which would have inhibited his breathing."

"And would that have made it easier for someone weaker to strangle him?" Ettie asked.

"A woman perhaps?" Elsa-May inquired before she'd reached the kitchen.

"That was my first thought, but logically, if someone was going to slip something to him, why not poison him outright then and there?"

"That's a very good point, Detective." Ettie said. "Maybe it would've implicated that person, if he'd dropped dead right next to the person who'd poisoned him."

"Thank you, Ettie," the detective said, his tone

full of sarcasm. “There are several scenarios that could be at play.”

“What was the drug?”

“Meperidene sold as demerol. Available only by prescription.”

“So what now?”

Kelly’s phone beeped and he pulled it out of his pocket and stared at it. “I just got a text message. My officers are five minutes away from the station and they’ve got Michael Skully with them. I have to go and ask some questions.”

“You’re not going to arrest him, are you?” Elsa-May asked sticking her head around the kitchen doorway.

“Depends on his answers.”

“Do you still have time for coffee?”

“I’ll have a quick one.”

It was several minutes after Detective Kelly left when Myra came to their door. The sisters had only just finished cleaning up the kitchen after the detective’s visit.

"They came to take Michael in for questioning. Do you know what it's about?"

"What did they tell you?" Ettie asked, following Myra as she flounced further into the house.

"It was something about those invitations. Before he left with the police, he told me he wrote them, but he was only trying to get you and me back on speaking terms, Mother."

"I'm sure there's nothing to worry about, then. As long as the truth is out, he's got nothing to worry about."

Myra collapsed onto the couch. "I hope you're right." She looked the two of them up and down. "Are you going somewhere?"

"We were, but not any more. Would you like a cup of coffee?"

"I suppose I need something."

Elsa-May went to the kitchen to make the coffee while Ettie sat down next to Myra. "Where and how did you meet Michael?"

"Does it matter?"

"Not really. I'm just trying to have a

conversation."

"Did I tell you before?"

Ettie looked up to the ceiling as she searched her mind. "I don't think you told me."

Myra shook her head in an agitated manner. "It doesn't matter now."

"What do you mean it doesn't matter now?"

"We met, we fell in love and we bought our house. We're building a life together. He's my soulmate."

"What kind of job does he do?"

"He's in sales."

"What does he sell?"

Myra recoiled from her mother. "Why all these questions?"

"I want to get to know him a little better."

"His job is just a job. He's not his job. That's something he does to get money. It says nothing about his personality or who he is as a person."

Ettie rubbed her chin. "It seems to me that a job is what people do with most of their waking hours. If you tell me what he does with those hours, I'll understand better what he does most of the time."

Myra breathed out heavily. "He sells pharmaceutical products. I'm certain I've told you this."

"Who to?"

"Doctors, hospitals—I guess."

"You don't know?"

"No! We've got better things to do with our time. He travels and makes good money. We've got a large mortgage. Houses like ours don't come cheap."

"It's a very nice house, I must say." Ettie realized their relationship was much more than Myra first described. They had bought a house together so it was more than just a boyfriend-girlfriend thing.

Elsa-May came back in the room. "Here we are." She handed a mug of coffee to Myra.

"Thank you," Myra said as she took the mug by the handle.

"Cookies?" Elsa-May asked.

"No, thank you." Myra took a sip of coffee.

"Myra was just telling me that Michael sells

pharmaceutical products."

Elsa-May's left eyebrow raised. "Drugs?"

Myra nodded. "Essentially, I suppose."

Ettie pressed her lips together. If *she'd* mentioned the word 'drugs,' Myra would've reacted far differently.

Chapter 11

As soon as Myra finished her coffee, she headed out the door to the police station to wait for Michael.

"What do you make of it, Elsa-May? She doesn't give much information away about Michael."

"I wonder if he's been in trouble with the police before."

"Kelly didn't mention anything of the kind."

"He probably doesn't tell us everything and he could like to have us think that he does."

Ettie pulled her mouth to one side. What her sister said was probably true. "I'd like to get to the bottom of it."

"We'll probably find out soon enough."

"Do you believe Michael's story about why he sent the invitations?"

"Not really. It seems a drastic thing to do to get mother and daughter to talk. Besides that, how could Myra and I have had a conversation with all the other people around?"

"That's right. You stay there and I'll wash up these things and then we can head off."

Later, when they were getting ready to head out the door again, they both jumped when someone thumped on the door.

Ettie and Elsa-May stared at each other.

"This is beginning to become a regular occurrence. I'm starting to think someone wants us to stay home today."

Ettie open the door to see their old friend, Ronald Crowley.

"Hello. I've just been talking to Myra. She was coming out of your house when I was heading toward it."

They stepped aside to allow him in.

"Come in out of the cold and take a seat," Elsa-May said.

"Would you like a cup of coffee?" Ettie asked.

He shook his head and sat down. "No, thank you."

Once they were all seated, Ettie asked, "Did

Myra tell you about her boyfriend?"

Elsa-May added, "He's been taken to the police station."

"Yes, she was very distressed. I offered to go with her, but she said she preferred to go alone."

"Have you two kept in contact?"

"We lost touch some time ago. That was her decision."

Elsa-May said, "She tells us that Michael admitted that he sent the invitations."

"Apparently he did that to get Myra and me talking to one another again," Ettie said.

"Do you believe that?" Elsa-May asked.

"Stranger things have happened," Crowley said.

Ettie pushed out her lips. "It seems unlikely to me."

"People do weird and wonderful things particularly around this time of year."

"Ettie and I were wondering if Michael had some kind of criminal history."

A hint of a smile twigged at the corners of Crowley's lips. "I already looked into that. I do have a few friends left on the force. Apart from a few speeding tickets there was nothing."

"Wasn't Detective Kelly asking you to help with this investigation?" Elsa-May asked.

"That's what he said originally, but I've heard nothing from him and he's not keeping me in the loop."

"Do you think Michael could've killed that man because he was annoying Myra?" Elsa-May asked.

"I can't say. We'd need more information."

Ettie continued, "If Michael didn't kill the man, who could've? I've had something running through my mind."

Crowley leaned forward. "What's that, Ettie?"

"Betsy Stoll—the young woman who had her life ruined by running away with Earl when she was a teenager. There is no going back to the community when you've run away with someone's husband. Well, she could've come back, but it would've been difficult for her."

"So she would've had a good motive? She wasn't at your Christmas party, though," Crowley said.

"No, she wasn't. I haven't seen her for many years."

"Not since she left the community," Elsa-May added.

"And do we know where she is now?"

Elsa-May and Ettie looked at each other and they both shook their heads.

"No. We haven't seen her, or heard about her, since she left the community," Elsa-May said.

"Detective Kelly asked us to talk with Moses Stoll and Naomi Fuller in a couple of days. They won't speak to Kelly now, and that's probably because they already told him all they know while they were here. Kelly asked us to wait a day or two and then go and see what we could find out, but before we do that we could find Betsy."

Crowley said, "I could drive you anywhere you want to go tomorrow."

"Tomorrow?" Elsa-May asked. "What's wrong with today?"

"I've got some things to do today. Tomorrow I'm free."

"Why don't we stay home today, Ettie, and we'll go out tomorrow?"

"I think that would be a good idea. Every time we try to head out, someone's at the door." Ettie giggled. "Now, Ronald, we've got some lovely orange cake left. Would you like to try some?"

His face lit up. "Does it have frosting?"

"Loads of it."

"Yes please. And while you're at it, I might take you up on that offer of coffee, Ettie."

"Of course."

"I'll just make a quick call to Kelly." Crowley took the phone out of his pocket and stepped outside the house.

"Ettie, with Ronald driving us tomorrow that will save us money on taxis."

"*Jah,* but he'll have to stay out of sight. We don't want anyone to be scared off and they might be if we're seen with a detective."

"He's a retired detective."

"He still looks like a detective."

Ettie giggled. "That's true, he does."

They placed coffee and cake down on the coffee table for the detective just as he stepped back inside the house.

"Any news from Detective Kelly?" Elsa-May asked as she sat down in her favorite chair and picked up her knitting from the bag by her feet.

He stared at the cake in front of him. "Michael made a statement that the people he sent the invitations to were people Myra had spoken to him about. That's how he came up with the list. Kelly is convinced he's guilty, but he's let him go for now until he gathers more evidence."

Ettie gasped. "Myra will be devastated if he did it."

"We'll have to hope that Myra is not named as an accessory to murder if he's found guilty." Crowley shook his head.

Elsa-May pointed to his cake. "Eat up. Everything looks brighter after cake."

Crowley sat down in front of his cake and coffee. "Thank you, this looks good."

Ettie asked, "Did Kelly say anything else?"

When Crowley had finished his mouthful, he said, “I told him that I would be driving both of you around to talk to people over the next couple of days. He said it wouldn’t hurt to keep asking questions. The danger is that Kelly might start to think that Myra was somehow involved.”

“We’ll have to find the real killer,” Elsa-May said.

Crowley nodded. “And fast.”

Chapter 12

The next morning, the two sat across from Moses, hoping he might know of his daughter's whereabouts.

"I don't have any idea where she's gone," Moses said in answer to their inquiry.

"What about her friends? Did she have a friend she might have kept in contact with?"

He shook his head. "It's not likely that she kept any friends around here after what she did."

Ettie's shoulders slouched.

"I tell you what I have. I have letters she wrote to a pen pal. I only came across them a week or two ago when I was throwing things out. When Betsy was a young girl she wasn't doing too well in *schul* and the teacher suggested that the children who were struggling with reading and writing should have a pen pal. Betsy wrote to that pen pal every week for years."

"Can we see those letters?" Elsa-May asked.

"I'll get them for you." He left them in the living room and came back with a box of letters.

Ettie sifted through them to see they were all from the same address. "I wonder if Betsy's kept in contact with this person?" Ettie looked for the name. "Roslyn Jones."

Elsa-May looked over her shoulder. "It's not too far away. We could drive there and knock on the door."

"Young Roslyn came here once."

"The girls met?"

He nodded. "They were about seventeen at the time."

"She was an *Englischer?*" Ettie asked.

"*Jah,* she was."

"Do you mind if we write down her address?" Elsa-May asked.

"I'll do you one better than that. You can take the box with you."

"How did you make out?" Crowley asked when they got back into the car.

"We've got a lead. A pen pal that Betsy had when she was living at home."

Elsa-May tapped on the box she had on her lap. "These are all of the pen pal's letters." Elsa-May handed the address to Crowley.

"Are you planning to knock on the door?"

"Yes," the sisters chorused.

"Okay. Let's do it," Crowley said, turning the key in the ignition.

When they arrived at the address on the envelopes, Elsa-May got out of the car while Ettie waited with Detective Crowley.

Minutes later, they watched Elsa-May head back to the car with a grin on her face and a piece of paper in her hand.

"She's got something," Ettie said.

"Let's hope so."

Elsa-May opened the door and slid into the backseat. "I've got it."

"Good work, Elsa-May. What did you get?"

"Her address. They still write to one another even

though they haven't seen each other in over twenty years. She was hesitant to give it to me at first until I told her about Earl. Roslyn thought Betsy would like to know about his death." Elsa-May handed Crowley the address.

"Betsy must have told Roslyn everything," Ettie said.

Crowley unfolded the paper. "It's about a twenty-minute drive away."

"That's not too bad," Elsa-May said.

Crowley programed the information into his car's GPS navigation system. "Okay, off we go."

When they pulled up at the address that Roslyn had given them, Ettie announced she would go in by herself.

When Ettie got closer to the three story red brick building, she was pleased to see that apartment number three was on the ground floor. She didn't fancy walking up stairs. That was something she avoided wherever possible.

Breathing heavily in front of apartment number

three, she raised her hand and knocked. She hoped for Betsy's sake that hearing the news about Earl wouldn't bring back too many bad memories.

The door opened and a small dark-haired woman stood before Ettie, pulling a sweater over her head. Her hair was tousled and she looked as though she'd just gotten out of bed. The woman was not Betsy.

"Hello, I'm sorry to disturb you, but I'm looking for Betsy."

"She's at work."

"I knew Betsy many years ago… I'm sorry, did I wake you?"

"I'm on the night shift. I work at the same hospital as Betsy."

"Arr, we just passed the hospital."

"Yes that's the one; it's nice and close. I know that Betsy used to be Amish, did you know her from then?"

"Yes, I did and I'm afraid I have some rather distressing news for her. Someone she knew has died."

"That Amish guy who died on Christmas day?"

"You know?"

"Betsy and I saw it in the papers. I know that he persuaded her to leave the Amish with him."

"I would like to talk about it with her. What time will she be home?"

"Her shift finishes at three, but you could try to catch her during her break at the hospital. Just ask at the front desk and they'll direct you."

"Thank you, I'll try to do that."

Ettie hurried back to the car to tell the others what she'd learned.

Chapter 13

Ettie walked into the hospital with Crowley towering over her to her right, and her sister on her left.

The three of them were heading to the main desk when Ettie noticed a sign pointing to the hospital cafeteria. "I don't know about the both of you, but I could do with something to eat right now."

"Why don't we do that, and then we can find Betsy after that?" Elsa-May asked.

"Whatever you ladies want. I'm just the driver."

Ettie and Elsa-May hurried into the café convinced that they couldn't go on without proper nourishment.

As they looked at the menu, they decided sandwiches and coffee would be the quickest option.

"Why don't you two find a table and I'll bring the food over?" Crowley suggested.

After arguments about who was going to pay,

Crowley managed to convince them he'd pay and he'd also bring the food back to them.

Ettie and Elsa-May sat at a table next to a floor to ceiling window that overlooked the parking lot. When Ettie managed to pull her eyes away from the bright orange plastic tablecloth she noticed a nurse who'd just walked in.

Ettie tugged at Elsa-May's sleeve. "Look! She looks like an older Betsy. Do you think that's her?"

"It looks like her. *Jah,* I think it is. Go over and talk to her, Ettie."

Ettie stood up and walked over to the lady and stood beside her.

When the woman looked at Ettie, she immediately recognized her. "Mrs. Smith?"

"Betsy?"

"Yes." Betsy leaned over and gave Ettie a hug.

"I don't remember you being quite so tall. Or maybe I've shrunk over the years."

"I've always been quite tall," Betsy said. "What brings you here?"

"Actually, you do."

Betsy's eyebrows pinched together. "Me?"

"Yes. Your roommate told us where you work." She nodded over at Elsa-May.

"You brought your sister?"

"Yes."

"I'll get something to eat and then say hello to her. Who is that man at the table? Is he with you?"

"He's just a friend who drove us here."

"Is my father all right? Is that why you've come?"

"He's okay. We're here because of Earl Fuller."

"I heard he died. Why are you here to see me? I don't think he was ever a patient here at the hospital."

"No, it's nothing to do with you being a nurse. Do you have a few minutes to sit down?"

"Yes. I'm on a break right now; I've got about ten minutes. I'll just get something to eat."

Ettie waited with Betsy while she got some food and then they sat down with Crowley and Elsa-May. Ettie introduced Betsy to Crowley after Betsy greeted Elsa-May.

"We were just wondering, when was the last time you've heard from him?" Elsa-May asked.

"Never. Not from the time I left him years ago."

Ettie figured she should offer some information of her own perhaps that would make her talk more freely. "Do you remember my daughter, Myra?"

"Yes, I know her. I knew her quite well. We were close once."

"Myra and Earl met each other again a couple of years ago and were friendly for a brief time and then it seems they quickly became enemies."

"Yes, and I would say none of that was Mrya's fault. Earl was good at making enemies out of friends."

"We're are just a bit concerned that since he was killed just outside my house that the police suspicions might turn on Myra. That's why we're here."

Elsa-May continued where Ettie left off, "And we were wondering if you might know of any enemies he had, or someone who might want to see him dead?"

"He probably wronged so many people over the years. There's his brother, Wayne. They never got along, but things might have changed from years ago. I remember Wayne left the community about a year before Earl."

"That's very helpful, thank you, Betsy. And do you know anything else about Wayne? Where we might be able to find him?"

"Sorry. I don't. How is everybody in the community? I haven't seen anyone."

"Your father is well."

"You know you could call in and see him sometime. He misses you."

"I know, but it's hard after what happened. I don't think anyone from the community would be pleased to see me. My father was always far too worried about appearances and what other people might think. I can imagine how much shame he felt when I ran away with a married man." She glanced at her wristwatch. "I have to go."

"We were pleased to see you, Betsy. It's been nice." Ettie smiled at Betsy remembering the young girl from many years ago.

"Not everybody in the community is like you two."

Elsa-May chuckled. "A couple of silly old fools?"

"Oh no, you're nothing like that at all. You're very nice people."

"You might be surprised how your father might react when he sees you, Betsy, if you pay him a visit. Sometimes it pays to give people a chance."

"A chance to be reminded how much I disappointed him," Betsy said.

"Sometimes we build up things in our minds when the reality is not half as bad as we think it's going to be."

Crowley said, "If you will excuse me, I'll go and get myself another cup of coffee. Anyone else want one?"

The three ladies at the table shook their heads.

When Crowley was gone, Betsy said, "I feel so ashamed of what I did. I was young and stupid. I'd never do anything like that now."

"Everyone makes mistakes, Betsy. It's hard when you're young to make good decisions. That's why the young need to listen to advice."

"Yes, but not many young people make mistakes so huge that they're ones they can't come back from."

"Is that why you stayed away from the community?"

"That and other reasons. I have many questions now about the beliefs. And from what I found, the bishop doesn't like people questioning things like the *Ordnung.*"

Elsa-May said. "There are a few things that need to be accepted by faith. Things are too high sometimes for our small minds to understand and fathom."

"I suppose that's true, but aren't we easily led astray when we're told to accept things by faith?"

Ettie pushed out her lips. "I know what you're saying seems right and we could talk about this for hours."

"You're right and I don't have the time right

now." She glanced at her watch again. "I might visit my father. I know he's getting on in age and I might run out of time."

Crowley sat back down with his second cup of coffee.

"Well that's my break, already over. It was really nice to see both of you, and nice to meet you too, Ronald." Betsy stood up.

"And you, Betsy," Detective Crowley said as he stood when she did.

When Betsy left the table and was out of earshot, Crowley sat back down, and said, "I just called the details about the brother through to Kelly."

"What details? She didn't have any details," Elsa-May said.

"She gave us a name. That's a good place to start. Kelly is running the name through the system."

Chapter 14

During the drive home from seeing Betsy Stoll, Kelly phoned Crowley. Crowley put his cell phone on speaker.

Ettie and Elsa-May heard how Earl's brother, Wayne Fuller, had a long criminal record and was currently in jail for armed robbery.

"Did you hear that?" Detective Crowley asked the sisters when he ended the call.

"Yes, we heard. So that means the brother didn't do it."

"Unless he had someone else do it for him," Elsa-May suggested.

"Yes, he could've, but why now? And what benefit was there in having his brother dead? Wayne wasn't named in the will. We'll need a lot more than that to persuade Kelly that Michael isn't guilty."

"What about hatred?" Elsa-May suggested. "I'm guessing he wasn't recently provoked since he's been incarcerated for the past five months."

"It's a mystery," Ettie said with a sigh.

"What do we do from here, Ronald?" Elsa-May asked.

"After I take you ladies home, I'm going to go down to the station and see where Kelly's up to with things. I'll see if he's got some forensic reports back yet. Maybe they found someone else's prints in his car or something that will give us a lead."

"What if Michael did it?" Ettie asked. "He was outside and had the opportunity and besides that he was the one who wrote the invitations. Maybe Kelly's right about him. Not only that, one of the police said it looked like he was trying to drive away. If it weren't for his car's battery being dead, he wouldn't be under arrest right now. He would've been long gone."

"I didn't like to say that before, Ettie, but I think you might be right. The only thing is where does Myra fit into his plans?"

Elsa-May said, "It is odd that he was in that street and claims he didn't see anyone else. He didn't see

Santa or the man who was killed. He should've at least seen those two people."

"He seemed confused," Crowley said.

Ettie said to Crowley, "Myra is innocent."

"Yes, I know she wouldn't have killed the man, but exactly how much did she know—if Michael was the one who killed Earl? Had they talked about killing the man in jest? Michael might turn around and say that Myra had asked him to do it or had some involvement somehow. That's what concerns me."

"We need to find out exactly what happened," Elsa-May said.

"I wonder when Earl's funeral will be," Ettie said to Elsa-May who merely shrugged her shoulders.

"We have to find out all we can. I'm still driving you to talk with people tomorrow, aren't I?"

"That would be wonderful if you could do that," Ettie said. "Before Kelly made the arrest he asked us to talk with Moses Stoll and Naomi Fuller, but to wait a day or two until we talked with them, and that would bring us up to tomorrow."

"Perfect timing," Elsa-May agreed.

"Except we've already gone to Moses about Betsy. Do you think we should go there again? We should've asked him more when we were there."

"I think it's fine to go back there," Elsa-May said. "We'll take him a cake."

"Perfect idea, Elsa-May. I'll bake one tonight."

* * *

Elsa-May and Ettie weren't home long when Ava came to the door.

"I don't have long," Ava said hurrying over to the couch.

"Why are you rushing so much, my girl?" Elsa-May asked Ava.

"Jeremiah and I have had such a busy time and so many visitors that we're just going to have a quiet night at home with just the two of us. I'm cooking something extra special for him."

"Ah, newlyweds."

"That sounds like a lovely idea,"

The sisters told Ava everything that had happened and everything they knew so far.

"Poor Myra, she must be devastated," Ava said. "And to think that the man was killed right outside on your property."

Ettie pulled a face. "Don't remind us of that."

"Are you going to the fireworks on New Year's Day?"

"What fireworks?" Ettie asked.

"There's going to be fireworks at Abraham Glick's place. New Years Day night, actually."

"They did that last year too," Elsa-May said.

Ettie smiled. "We might go and stay for a little while."

"I can take you there and bring you home if you like. I'll drive you home whenever you want to go."

"Then we'll definitely go. *Denke,* Ava," Elsa-May said.

Ava asked, "So who do you think could've done it if it wasn't Myra's boyfriend?"

"Well, there's always a reason. People don't go

around killing people for no reason at all, so the man must've caused someone some grief."

Ettie raised her eyebrows. "We've learned that he caused many people grief over the years. It could've been any one of those people."

"And for all we know, we probably don't know half of the people who had wanted him gone."

"Detective Kelly is checking into his business associates."

"Hopefully he'll know more soon."

Ava stood up. "It's time I made a move. I'll collect you just as it's starting to get dark for the fireworks."

"Very good."

"*Denke*, Ava."

* * *

Ettie and Elsa-May hadn't heard from Myra, and when Crowley arrived the next day to take them to visit Moses and Naomi, he informed them that he'd had a few distressed calls from Myra since he'd left them the day before.

"I hope she's okay," Ettie commented.

"We were on the phone for a long time last night and again this morning. She's okay. Michael's moved out, saying he can't trust her. She questioned him about the incident and he took offense."

Ettie pushed out her lips wishing Myra might have come to her instead of turning to Crowley for comfort.

"Ettie, we have to focus on finding out what really happened. Kelly is looking into people Michael knew from his job, trying to find more proof of his guilt. While he's doing that, we'll find out what we can from your Amish friends."

Ettie nodded and Elsa-May patted her on the shoulder.

"Let's get this done, Ettie," Elsa-May said, now picking tiny pieces of lint off Ettie's black shawl.

Ettie slapped her hand away. "Stop it!"

"Are we ready?" Crowley asked, standing up and staring at the two of them.

"Yes," Ettie said, walking out the door first with

a tin containing a chocolate cake.

"I'll just make sure that I've got enough water out for Snowy."

"We'll wait in the car," Crowley said. While he walked with Ettie, he asked her to tell him about Moses, the first person on the list to visit.

"Moses has a large farm, which two of his boys now run for him. He lives in the *grossdaddi haus,* which is built onto the main farmhouse. You would've probably seen all that from yesterday. But what you don't know is, his wife died before his children were fully grown leaving him with five boys and the youngest child, Betsy, who was the only daughter."

"Well, that sums it up nicely."

"I can't think of much more to tell you than that. If I had to guess, I'd say he was in his seventies."

Chapter 15

"Where should I park?" Crowley asked when he pulled onto Moses Stoll's farm.

"Just park under this tree here. We don't want him to see you. He'll ask who you are."

Ettie and Elsa-May walked up to the front door of the *grossdaddi* house and Elsa-May knocked. After waiting a moment, she was about to knock again when the door was flung open.

"Hello again. This is a nice surprise."

Much to Ettie's horror, Elsa-May got right to the point. "We're here to talk about what happened the other night."

"We've brought you chocolate cake," Ettie said, hoping to soften Elsa-May's words.

He opened the door wider. "I love cake of any kind. Chocolate is always my first preference. How did you know, Ettie?"

"I just guessed."

"Come into the living room. We can eat cake

with a cup of tea."

After he showed them to the living room, they sat on a small couch, while Moses pulled a chair out from the dining table nearby to sit on.

"Would you like a cup of tea or would you prefer *kaffe?"*

"Nee, don't go to any bother for us," Ettie said. "Don't waste any cake on us."

"And we just had tea at home, so we'll get right to the point," Elsa-May said.

"That's often the best way," he said.

Ettie took over knowing her approach would be softer than her sister's. "Myra is concerned that someone is trying to make it look like she killed Earl. She knew him and they didn't get along."

"That's no good. Who would do that?" Moses asked.

"We don't know, but we're trying to figure it out and you could help us by answering some questions."

He nodded. "I'll help all I can."

"Denke."

Elsa-May took over. "When was the last time you saw Earl?"

"When he was dead at your house. I looked out the window."

"And, before that?"

"I didn't see him after he took Betsy away from me. I had no word from him or Betsy after that. I heard that things hadn't worked out between them and things ended between them. That's all I know. Betsy knows where I am. I haven't moved from this house. And yet, she's not been back to see me, or her brothers. She's missed all her brothers' weddings and I can't count how many nieces and nephew she hasn't met." He shook his head and looked as though he was fighting back tears.

"I know this must be very hard for you. "

"I see Myra's talking to you, Ettie?" he said.

Ettie pouted. "It appears I only see her when she has trouble in her life."

"Still, that means something. She knows where to turn when things get rough in her life. She has some kind of trust in you."

Ettie's eyebrows wiggled. She hadn't thought of it like that. Perhaps it was a good thing Myra came to her even if she was rude and condescending most of the time.

Moses continued, "My greatest hope for all my *kinner* was that they would have been with me in eternity in *Gott's haus.* Where will Betsy end up?" He looked down at his hands. "Rachel wouldn't have been able to go through this if she'd still been alive. Betsy brought shame upon our *familye.* As time fades away, the feeling of shame has also faded."

"It's not too late. Something is never over until it's over." Ettie didn't like to give him false hope by telling him that she'd seen his daughter yesterday and she was well, had a job, and was a useful member of the community. She could only hope that Betsy had listened to what she and Elsa-May had to say and would soon visit her father.

Elsa-May coughed. "We can only show them the right way. It's up to them to choose."

"I tell myself that, Elsa-May, but it doesn't make it any easier."

Ettie reminded herself to concentrate on the reason they were there, and that was to find out about Earl. "I believe one of Earl's brothers left the community a little before he did and he's been in trouble with the law."

"I heard rumours. I don't know anything about it."

Ettie tried to think of what the detective would ask him if he was there.

"When you were at our place on Christmas day, did you see anyone go outside and come back in just before Santa Claus rushed into the house?"

He scratched his head. "Yes, I thought I saw Naomi go out. And I only noticed that because every time the front door opened a cold gust of wind would blow right through the house."

"Interesting," Ettie said she looked over at Elsa-May. "Did you tell the detectives that?"

"*Nee,* I didn't want her getting into any trouble."

Ettie and Elsa-May, made their way back to Crowley's car.

"What have you learned?" he asked.

"Quite a lot," Elsa-May answered.

Ettie took over, "He told us he saw Naomi go outside and come back in sometime before Santa rushed into the house."

"Was he sure?" Crowley asked.

"That's just it. He said he wasn't sure and he didn't mention it to the police because he didn't want to get Naomi into trouble."

"What else?" Crowley asked.

"He hasn't seen his daughter since she left the community and he knows nothing about Earl or his brother."

"Where to now?"

"You tell me."

"Naomi Fuller's house."

"What's her address?"

When Ettie told him, he programed it into the GPS.

"There was no need to do that. It's just to the

left, to the right and to the right again."

Elsa-May added, "It's only about a mile away."

Crowley chuckled. "It's a habit. Now tell me a little of Naomi's background."

"Well, you know that Earl ran away with Moses' daughter, then Naomi had to take in sewing to support herself. At one time she was working at a local dressmaker's and now I think she works from home."

Soon Ettie and Elsa-May were greeting Naomi at her front door. "Nice to see both of you." She glanced out the door and saw the car. "Is that the man from the other night?"

"It's the retired detective. He's an old friend and he's driven us here."

"He was also a friend of Myra's," Ettie added.

"Does he want to come inside? It'll be cold out there in the car."

Elsa-May waved a hand through the air. "He won't mind."

"We can sit in the kitchen." She showed them to the kitchen and with a sweep of her hand moved all the sewing on the table to one side. "Have a seat. Sorry about all this mess."

"No need to be sorry at all," Elsa-May said as she sat down at the table.

"We didn't mean to interrupt you," Ettie said following Elsa-May's lead and sitting down at the other side of the table.

"That's okay. I'm running ahead of schedule. I work from home nowadays."

Ettie nodded. "We heard you did."

"Would you like a cup of hot tea?"

"We'd love one thanks." Elsa-May answered for both of them.

Because Crowley was waiting for them in the car Ettie thought she better get quickly to the point before her sister did. "Naomi, I've heard you're coming into quite a bit of money."

Naomi chuckled. "I suppose that's a good thing. I won't know what to do with it. It hardly makes up for what he did to me." She sat down at the table after she'd put the pot on to boil. "Money won't get me back all the lost years and it won't bring me *kinner* or a husband. He took all that away from me. "

"At least now you'll be able to get married again," Elsa-May said.

"I've no interest in things like that now, not at my age. I'm too old and cranky and set in my ways."

Ettie nodded looking at Elsa-May. "I know what that's like."

Elsa-May narrowed her eyes at Ettie.

Naomi sighed. "It's left to me to do the funeral and it's on in three days. I'm not having a viewing here at the *haus*. He's not having an Amish funeral in any way. The body's at the funeral director's and then will be taken to the graveyard. Bishop John was kind enough to say that he'd read something and say a prayer by the grave." She shook her head. "I've got no idea what kind of things the bishop can say since we know where Earl's not going."

"He'll be tactful, don't worry. And we'll be there to support you."

"Oh, I'm not worried. It would be better if he weren't tactful. It's funny, after all these years, that it's up to me to give him a funeral."

"Apparently he never made another will or his own arrangements for a funeral, or anything."

"Probably too busy doing other things like making life a misery for everyone he came into contact with," Naomi said.

"Or, he always saw you as his wife and the community as his home," Elsa-May said tactfully.

"Don't make him out to be something that he's not, Elsa-May. People always think they have to say nice things about people when they're dead. He was a liar from the start and I only found that out after we were married. But that's what *Gott* wanted me to go through and I've gone through it and I've come out of it. I won't say I'm not bitter; I have to learn forgiveness."

Naomi got out of her chair when she heard the water boiling. When she'd made the tea, she poured out three cups.

"And did you ever see him after he left you?" Ettie asked.

"The last time I ever saw him was the day he

left."

Ettie took a sip of tea, and then placed the cup in the saucer. "When you came to our place the other night, did you go outside at any time and come back again, before Santa Claus burst into the house?"

"*Nee,* I didn't. Why?"

"No reason."

"I told the police that already."

"Did you see anyone go outside at all and then come back in?"

"Funny you should ask because I'm certain I noticed Moses go outside, and I don't remember seeing him come back in. He must've, though because the next thing I remember was Santa Claus bursting through the door."

Ettie and Elsa-May stared at each other. Now they had both Moses and Naomi saying they each saw the other leave the house.

Elsa-May said, "I don't suppose you know anything of Wayne, your *bruder*-in-law?"

"You mean have I heard from him?"

Elsa-May nodded.

"*Nee.* I heard he got into some kind of trouble. Earl didn't like to talk about him. They didn't get along and Earl never said why." She sighed. "Do you know we were only married six months before he left?"

"Was that all?" Ettie asked.

Naomi nodded.

They walked back to the car and told Crowley what they'd learned.

"With the funeral on in three days, the police must already have the coroner's report and all the forensic tests back," Elsa-May said.

"Hmm, I'll make a call to Kelly later and see what I can find out. It's odd that they each—Moses and Naomi—think that the other left your house before the man was killed. Neither of them mentioned it when Kelly was questioning them."

"We know," Ettie said. "They were possibly trying to protect one another."

"It sounds more like each was trying to implicate the other, but why do that now? Why not when we were asking the questions?"

"They've had time to think about it?" Ettie asked.

Crowley's phone sounded. He had it on speaker at the start but as soon as he heard it was Myra he switched the speaker off. Ettie was concerned because she sounded upset.

"It's okay. Yes, I'll come over now. I'll be as quick as I can." He ended the call. "Myra."

"We know," Elsa-May said.

"She's quite distressed." He started the car. "I'll take both of you home and then I'll go and see her."

"Has anything else happened?" Ettie asked.

"Yes. Michael has left her." Crowley drove back down the driveway.

Ettie opened her mouth but didn't know what to say. She didn't know Michael well enough to know if he was a good man for her daughter or not. "I'm glad you'll be there to comfort her and give her advice."

Elsa-May said, “When you see Myra, tell her that Earl’s funeral is on in three days.”

“I doubt she’ll want to go, but I’ll tell her,” he said.

Chapter 16

Ettie reluctantly got ready for the celebrations at Abraham's farm. She didn't want to tell Elsa-May she'd prefer not going. Her sister seemed rather keen on the idea. All Ettie wanted was a quiet night with her needlework in front of the fire. If only Elsa-May would get a hurry on with that new shawl.

For a change, Ettie was the first to be ready while Elsa-May fussed over Snowy. Ettie wandered over to the widow when she heard a bird's call. The night was lit with a nearly full moon and Ettie watched some birds she figured were flying home.

"Where do the birds go when it snows?" Ettie called out.

Elsa-May looked up from pulling one of Snowy's knitted sweaters on him. "I'm not certain. I suppose many of them find shelter in barns or roofs."

"*Jah,* I would think they'd need more shelter than just having a nest in a tree."

"Maybe I could knit some bird sweaters with that brown wool you gave me."

Ettie whipped her head around to look at her sister. "That's not funny, Elsa-May. You know that's for my shawl."

Elsa-May chuckled and straightened up while Snowy ran off in his blue and white sweater that Elsa-May had knitted him out of left over wool.

"Oh, it sounds like they're here," Elsa-May said.

"I was ready first." Ettie was pleased with herself for being ready twenty minutes early. They'd eaten dinner early and cleaned the kitchen, ready for a rare night out.

"I'll leave Snowy inside and leave his dog door unlatched."

"That would make sense," Ettie commented.

When they walked out to the waiting buggy, they were surprised to see that Jeremiah wasn't there. Ava sat tall in the driver's seat holding onto the leather reins.

"Where's Jeremiah?" Elsa-May asked as she climbed into the buggy.

"He was tired so he's staying home."

Ettie climbed in after Elsa-May and swallowed her complaints about Jeremiah doing what she wanted to do.

"Don't forget, I'll take you home whenever you're ready."

"We'll let you know. *Denke,* Ava," Ettie said. Ava would be more keen to leave early with Jeremiah at home, Ettie figured.

"How's the murder investigation going?" Ava asked as she turned the buggy around to head back down the road.

Elsa-May sighed. "Michael has left Myra because she questioned him about the other night. We've talked with Naomi and Moses and each say they saw the other leave the house just before Earl was found dead."

"*Jah,* and Crowley is wondering why they're saying that now, and kept quiet about it when the police were asking them questions."

"Maybe they were in it together," Ava suggested.

"That makes no sense." Elsa-May shook her

head. “If they were, they’d hardly say they saw the other gone.”

“That’s true.” Ava sighed. “I wish I’d been there that night. Maybe I would’ve seen something or heard something.”

“We need to find out who did it. Crowley says if we don’t, Michael might get arrested and somehow drag Myra into it because Earl was the one who was harassing Myra.”

Ava sighed. “I hope Myra is going to be okay.”

Ettie added, “She’s leaning on Crowley at the moment. He seems to calm her down. Hopefully, Detective Kelly can find out more from his investigations into Michael.”

The night was a blur for the sisters. The Glicks’ house and yard were full of people. The trees were decorated with glowing lanterns and everyone was either laughing or talking loudly.

There were games, happy faces and so much food. Ettie and Elsa-May had their fill of pork and sauerkraut and were ready to leave after two hours.

Ava managed to persuade them to wait a little longer so they could see the fireworks.

It didn't escape Ettie's notice that Naomi and Moses were nowhere to be seen.

Chapter 17

"Hurry up with that cup of hot tea, Ettie. We can't be late for a funeral no matter whose it is! You'll have to help wash those dishes and finish getting dressed. They'll be here any minute and I don't want to come home to see dirty dishes in the sink."

Ettie ignored her sister and peacefully sipped her hot tea from her new rosebud teacup. It seemed odd to be going to a funeral around Christmas and New Year.

"Elsa-May, have you noticed that not many people die around Christmas and New Year?"

Elsa-May stuck her head around the kitchen door to look at Ettie on the couch. "I hadn't really thought about that before. It's true, we don't go to many funerals around this time."

"Maybe we have some control over when we die."

"I doubt that very much."

"Perhaps *Gott* is too busy, or takes a break Himself."

"Don't be silly, Ettie. You shouldn't say things like that."

"He could be taking an inventory on who's moving in throughout the coming year." Ettie glanced over to see Elsa-May shaking her head at her. "Alright, I suppose I better get ready so we can arrive before everybody else."

"She's early," Elsa-May said when there was a knock on the door. "I told you to be ready. You go and fix yourself up. I'll let Ava in and I'll do your share of the washing up."

While Elsa-May hurried to let Ava in, Ettie left her tea and went to her room. All she had to do was fix her hair.

Ettie was halfway through brushing her hair when she heard Ava.

"Are you ready, Ettie?"

Now she had Ava hurrying her as well as her annoying sister. She glanced over to see Ava standing in the doorway with her hands on her hips.

"Would you like me to help you?" Ava asked.

Ettie passed her the brush. "I won't say no."

Ava took up the brush and finished brushing out Ettie's long gray hair. "How do you want it braided?"

"Just in one braid."

After she had finished Ettie's hair, she said, "I'll leave it to you to pin."

"Denke, Ava."

"Jeremiah's waiting in the buggy and you know how we hate to be late."

"I know. I've had Elsa-May nagging me all morning, but at this rate we're going to be the first ones there."

"That's the way Jeremiah likes it."

Ettie sighed as she placed her prayer *kapp* on her head. "Earl's being buried in the same graveyard as the Amish and the Mennonites. I doubt he'd want to be buried there. It seemed he lived his life without two thoughts to where he'd rest and who would have to give him a funeral."

"Only because he didn't make alternative

arrangements. It's ironic too, that Earl ran out on Naomi and now she has to give him his funeral. I wouldn't be too happy if I was Naomi. That's why she never smiles."

"Earl probably never thought about dying. When *Gott* finally comes to take me home I might have to ask Him what took Him so long."

"Ettie, don't say things like that. I don't like to think about you or Elsa-May being gone. I wouldn't know what to do without you."

While Ava stood there watching Ettie carefully tie the strings of her *kapp,* Ettie told her the latest information she'd learned.

Elsa-May stuck her head in the room. "Come on you two. There's no time for chin wagging. Jeremiah and I are waiting."

"All finished now and ready to go," Ettie said.

"Finally. And now we're ten minutes late," Elsa-May growled.

"You mean ten minutes later than you wanted to be, which will still make us ten minutes early."

Just before they arrived at the graveyard, Jeremiah asked, "Is Myra going to be here?"

"Nee, she didn't get along with Earl. She wouldn't come."

When they pulled up, they saw that they weren't the first ones there. There were two Amish buggies and a police car.

"I wonder what's going on?" Ava said. "Why is a police car here?"

"There's someone in handcuffs I think," Ettie said.

Elsa-May strained her eyes. "That's Wayne, Earl's *bruder,* the one who was in prison. They must've let him out for the funeral."

"I thought you said they never got along, Ettie," Ava said.

"That's right they didn't. Everyone knows they didn't get along."

Jeremiah said, "He gets a day out of jail, so he took it, I guess."

The other two buggies in the yard belonged to the bishop and Naomi.

"I must hurry over and speak with Naomi," Ettie said.

"I wonder if we're allowed to speak with Wayne," Jeremiah commented.

"Nee," Ava said. "I mean, probably not. You don't know him, do you?"

"Nee, but I know some of his cousins."

Elsa-May said, "I'll try to speak with him later, and see if he knows anything."

"That wouldn't be likely, Elsa-May. The man's been in prison for months," Ava commented.

Ettie was in rare agreement with her sister. "It doesn't hurt to ask."

Chapter 18

The graveyard was a familiar place to Ettie. This was where all her relatives were buried, her mother, her father and her dear husband. There was a strange sense of peace found at the resting place of those she held most dear.

She stood for a moment outside the buggy listening to the chatter coming from Elsa-May as she prattled on about one thing and another to her grandson and his wife. The sun was doing it's best to peep through the gray and white fluffy clouds. Even though there was no clear sunshine, the glare caused Ettie to squint.

Looking over her shoulder, Ettie saw Wayne. He caught her eye and gave her a nod. She smiled and nodded back, remembering him as an innocent child. He'd been skinny, dark-haired and freckle-faced—always polite with a ready smile. Life had taken a turn for the man. Perhaps it had been one wrong decision that tipped the scales of his life on the side of the wrong. What would cause someone raised in the community to take up a life of crime?

"You alright, Ettie?" Jeremiah asked.

She turned to see that everyone was now out of the buggy and more people were arriving. "Just lost in my own thoughts."

"Weren't you going to speak with Naomi?"

"I am."

"If you want to speak with her, it might be a good idea to do so now, before more people get here."

Ettie nodded and made her way to Naomi who was standing by herself next to the pine coffin by the open grave.

"Naomi!"

"Ettie, hello."

"How are you feeling?"

"I'll be glad when this day is over."

Ettie glanced up to see Elsa-May close to Wayne and looking as though she was about to talk to him. "It's good of you to give him a funeral."

"There was no one else."

Ettie nodded. "I suppose you saw that Wayne is

over there?"

"Jah, I called the prison. I thought Wayne should be here and they allowed him out."

"That was good."

"Earl wronged a great many people."

Ettie nodded again.

"It wasn't just me, but I dare say I was the one who suffered the most."

After she searched her mind for some comforting words, Ettie found none. "I don't know what to say, Naomi. I know you've been wronged and your life didn't turn out how you thought it would."

"Denke, Ettie." She wiped away a tear with the back of her hand. "It's nice that someone acknowledges what I've gone through. Many people tell me it's *Gott's* will, but I find that hard to take. That would mean that *Gott* wanted me to suffer, and why would He? It wonders me how some suffer things in life while some don't."

Ettie shrugged her shoulders. "What you say is true and I have no answers." It was no time for Ettie to ask the woman questions. Ettie put her arm around Naomi's shoulder while Naomi quietly sobbed. If Naomi was younger she might have been interested in marrying again, but she was now in her fifties and too old to have her own children. Still, maybe another man would be the very thing that could brighten Naomi's outlook on life. The woman was still young enough, compared to Ettie.

"I must pull myself together. I can cry tomorrow."

Ettie patted her on the back. "You'll feel better soon."

A moment later, a crowd of people surrounded Naomi, each trying to say a few words. Ettie stepped back and looked at Wayne to see that he was now walking closer to the grave with two officers in brown uniforms, one on either side. Then, out of the corner of her eye, she noticed movement. It was Elsa-May standing by Jeremiah's buggy waving her over.

Ettie hurried over to her sister. "What did you find out? Would they let you speak with him?"

"Jah."

"Well, what did he say?"

"He said that in the last five months they'd made amends. Earl had even told Wayne that he could stay with him when he got out if he promised to go straight."

"Oh! That is a surprise."

"There's more."

Ettie leaned closer.

"Earl told him that Myra had stolen his business idea and was trying to kill him."

Ettie's jaw dropped open. "Well, that's just rubbish."

"I'm just repeating what he said."

"Well, you don't believe it, do you?"

"Nee. I don't. Of course, I don't, but there must be a reason he said it. Why would he want us to think that Myra was trying to kill Earl?"

Ettie thought for a moment. "We should get Kelly to look into the prison records to see if Earl visited him like he said. He might be making it up."

"We could do that and that's probably a good idea, but how would he know about Myra and the business idea if he hadn't heard it from Earl?"

"Here's Kelly now and that looks like Crowley in the car with him."

When Kelly pulled up at the end of a row of buggies, Elsa-May and Ettie were right there to fill them in on what Wayne had said to Elsa-May.

"I'll look into things." He looked over at the grave. "Looks like they're about to get started."

Ettie and Elsa-May walked over to the grave first, followed by Kelly and Crowley who stayed back from the crowd. Wayne also stayed at a distance from the crowd.

The bishop opened his bible and read out two scriptures. After he'd finished, two men took up shovels and filled in the grave while the bishop read the words of a hymn in German.

There was little sense of peace here, unlike at other Amish funerals. The man had not kept to his faith and had gone astray. Ettie hated to think where he'd end up. Following God's ways in the brief time on earth seemed a small price to pay for eternity. If only the man hadn't ruined Naomi's life in the process of losing his own life to the world.

Ettie glanced over at Naomi who was on the other side of Elsa-May. She seemed to be taking things well and had hardened herself against the bitterness her husband had brought her.

When the last shovel of dirt was thrown into the grave, people turned and walked away. Ettie hurried to the detective who was walking up ahead with Crowley. "Detective Kelly."

He swung around. "Yes, Mrs. Smith?"

"Are you going to find out if Earl visited his brother?"

"Yes, I said I would." The detective chuckled. "I can't see that anyone would kill anyone over opening a spa."

"It was a wellness center," Crowley corrected him.

"Well, whatever it's called I don't think that would give anyone motive to…"

Crowley interrupted, "Why would Wayne say it? Wayne is trying to put blame onto Myra. We need to find out why he's doing that."

Kelly rubbed his chin and he glanced over at

Wayne. "You two stay here." He walked over to Wayne and his guards.

"How's Myra?"

He nodded. "She's feeling a little better, but she's still quite worried about the outcome of things."

"Do you think Michael's guilty?"

"It's hard to say. He was right there and he had the best opportunity out of anyone. And, he had the motive; getting rid of the man that was harassing his girlfriend."

Ettie looked over at Kelly to see Wayne talking to him. If only she was close enough to hear what was being said. "Has Santa remembered anything else?"

"They let him go the next morning after he was at your house. They drove him back to the institution and I don't think anyone's talked with him since."

Giving a quick look back at Kelly, Ettie asked, "Do you think it would be okay with Detective Kelly if you and I paid him a visit?"

"Yes, I don't think he'd mind. He doesn't think he's got any more information, and given the man's mental condition anything he says won't have much bearing in a court of law." Crowley chuckled. "Especially if he wore his Santa suit."

Ettie had to laugh with him; she had to agree.

Kelly walked back to them and Ettie noticed that Wayne was being led back to a car.

"What did he say?" Ettie asked Kelly.

"The same thing you said, Ettie. We'll check the prison records to see if his brother visited him."

Ettie nodded. "Good. And Crowley and I were wondering if you'd mind if we visited Santa."

"It's a bit late now isn't it? You're supposed to visit him before Christmas." Kelly laughed at his own joke.

Glancing at Crowley, who remained straight-faced, Ettie wondered if she should laugh. "The Santa in the institution," Ettie explained.

"I know what you mean, Mrs. Smith. I was just making a little joke."

Very little, Ettie thought. "Well, would it be okay if we visited the man?"

Kelly glanced at Crowley. "If you don't mind

accompanying Mrs. Smith I don't see that it would do any harm."

Crowley nodded. "I'd be happy to."

"Good."

"Shall we do that tomorrow?" Crowley asked Ettie.

Ettie nodded. "Tomorrow sounds good to me."

"I'll call the facility and make the arrangements."

Chapter 19

Ettie and Crowley were shown to Santa Claus, who was in the dayroom with the other patients.

Even though he wasn't wearing his Santa suit, he stood out with his flowing white beard and bushy white eyebrows. He wore brown pants, and a long-sleeved shirt was stretched over his large tummy. When they sat down at the table with him, his bright blue eyes fairly sparkled.

"Hello again, Ettie and Ronald. It's nice of you to visit me."

"We're here to find out about what you saw or heard the night—Christmas night—when you came across the dead man."

"Earl Fuller," Santa said.

"That's right."

"He had a brother, Wayne. He was a good boy."

Ettie gasped. "You know Wayne?"

"It's been in the papers," Crowley whispered to

Ettie.

"Yes, Wayne Fuller. He was a good boy, but he grew up and was too old for me to watch over. The Amish never allowed my visits, but I still watched over the Amish kiddies."

Crowley rubbed his nose. "Tell me everything you remember from that night when you were in Mrs. Smith's street."

"The street was dark and eerie. The only lights were coming from within the households. A car drove past me slowly. The driver stared at me and kept going."

"Did the car stop?" Ettie asked.

"The car stopped up ahead, did a U turn and then parked on the other side of the road."

"Then what?" Crowley asked.

"I started at the first house, knocked on the door and asked for donations."

"Then?"

"They gave me two dollars." He smiled, inflating his rosy cheeks some more.

"And then?" Crowley asked.

"I thanked the man and kept going."

"Did the man get out of the car?" Ettie asked.

"I heard two car doors open and shut. Moments later, two doors opened and shut again and after that, one door opened and shut. I didn't think anything of it at the time."

"Two doors shut, two doors shut again, and then only one shut?"

"Yes."

"Were they close together, or did you hear them far apart?" Crowley asked.

"It sounded like there was two people if that's what you're asking me. But, at the end only one got out of the car. Unless they just opened and closed it while staying in the car."

Crowley took a pad and pen out of his inner coat pocket and jotted some notes. "Go on."

"After the second lot of doors opening and closing, before the single door opened and closed, I heard a whir like someone was trying to start their car. It went on for a while as I was talking to the man at the door of his house. Then I heard a car door open and then slam."

"And that was the single door opening and closing?" Ettie asked.

"I'm guessing that's what happened. I was with one of your neighbors at the time, Ettie, getting a small donation. I left that house and kept walking up the street."

"The car was still there?" Ettie asked.

"Yes. And he was still sitting in the car and now he was trying to start it."

"Did you tell Detective Kelly this at any time?"

"He never asked. The police found him anyway, when they arrived."

"He was the one the police were pulling out of the car?" Crowley asked.

"Yes, that was Michael Skully."

"You're good at remembering names," Crowley said.

He stared at Crowley, "Comes with the territory."

"So the man could've got out of his car, walked to Ettie's house and then got back in the car?"

Santa nodded. "The man would've had plenty of

time to do that."

Ettie and Crowley stared at each other.

"Thank you. You've been very helpful," Crowley said to Santa.

He put out his hand. "Can you spare a donation for charity?"

Crowley smiled and pulled out a few coins from his pocket and placed them carefully in Santa's chubby hand.

Santa closed his hand around the coins, and with his other hand, he grabbed Crowley's hand. "Thank you. You've always been a good boy, Ronald."

"Thank you, you've been very helpful," Ettie said pushing herself to her feet.

"Goodbye. You've always been a favorite of mine, too, Ettie."

They left Santa sitting at the little table and when they made their way out of the room, a nurse approached them. "How was your visit?"

"He believes he's Santa," Crowley said as though he was still trying to take it in.

"He has an uncanny memory," the nurse said.

"Yes, he seems to remember everyone's names," Ettie said.

"Not only names. He has a memory for everything. The doctors first thought he had some kind of savant syndrome, but now they think it's hyperthymesia and, besides that, he possibly had a traumatic episode happen in his past around Christmas time."

"I've heard of savant syndrome," Crowley explained to Ettie. "That's where someone with a disability displays some kind of extraordinary ability such as playing the piano brilliantly when they haven't learned." He turned back to the nurse. "What is the other condition you mentioned?"

"Hyperthymesia. Someone with that condition can tell you all about their life in specific detail. They'll know what day of the week their fifth birthday was on, for example, and facts like that."

"How does that work in his case, since he's convinced he's Santa?"

"His is a complex case and they're still trying to determine exactly what he's afflicted with. They doctors here have differing opinions. Their latest conclusion is that he has a few syndromes crossing over each other—something associated with the traumatic episode I was talking about."

Crowley rubbed his chin. "Has he ever displayed violence?"

"Oh no! He's as gentle as you'd expect the real Santa Claus to be."

"Has he ever slipped out of his Santa Claus routine?"

The nurse shook her head. "He hasn't. I could set up a meeting with one of his doctors for you. They'd be able to tell you more."

"Can we get back to you on that?" Crowley asked.

"Of course."

Crowley and Ettie left the building.

"What do you think?" Ettie asked.

"He's got a good memory, that's how he's able to remember everyone's names. And he can definitely remember details of the other night."

"Like the car in my street."

"Yes, but we're no closer to knowing the truth of what happened. I'll make a call and see where Kelly's gotten to with things."

Ettie and Crowley walked to Crowley's car while he spoke on his mobile phone with Kelly. Once they reached the car, Crowley ended the call.

"He's got nothing?" Ettie asked.

"It seems that Michael had been fired from his job six months ago."

"Really?"

"Yes. That makes things look worse for him."

"How's that?"

"He was lying to Myra about that, which makes me wonder what else was he lying about? Where was he on those 'business trips?' According to Myra, he was away a fair bit."

"Yes, she told me that too. Did Kelly ask him?"

"Michael will no longer cooperate. He's getting a lawyer."

Chapter 20

"I should take Snowy for a walk. He hasn't been on one for a few days."

"*Jah,* and maybe that will stop him from chewing my slippers," Ettie said.

Elsa-May frowned. "He hasn't done that for weeks now, has he?"

Ettie raised her left foot to reveal a toeless slipper. Elsa-May put her hand over her mouth and laughed.

"I'll come on the walk with you to keep you company."

"Okay, but don't take forever to get ready."

"All I have to do is put on my boots and coat."

"Snowy and I'll wait for you by the front door."

While they walked in the cool morning air, they discussed who might be responsible for the death of Earl Fuller. They didn't come up with any new scenarios, and just when they were on the home stretch, they saw a white car pull up outside their house. Someone walked up to their front door.

"Who could that be?" Elsa-May asked, squinting to see the driver.

"It's a young woman."

When they got closer, Elsa-May said, "It's Roslyn, Betsy's pen pal."

"Why is she here?"

"I gave her our address."

"Why did you do that?"

"She was hesitant to give me Betsy's address, so I gave her ours."

"You didn't tell me that."

"I don't need to tell you everything."

Ettie and Elsa-May came up behind Roslyn as she knocked on their door.

"Hello, Roslyn," Elsa-May said.

She swung around. "Oh, hello. Have I caught you heading out or coming home?"

"We just finished walking the dog," Ettie said.

"Are you here with news of Betsy?" Elsa-May asked. "We spoke with her at the hospital where she worked."

"I thought there is something you might like to know about Betsy."

Elsa-May and Ettie looked at one another.

"I'll put on a pot of tea, and we'll sit by the fire," Ettie said.

"I'll put Snowy outside while you put the pot on to boil, Ettie. Roslyn, make yourself comfortable by the fire."

When they were all sitting in the living room in front of a raging fire with hot tea, Roslyn began, "The last few letters I got from Betsy were all about Earl. She was being obsessive. I was worried. She asked me if I could help her find out where he was. I refused and told her that the way he'd treated her she shouldn't be interested. She hadn't mentioned him for years and I hoped she wasn't trying to reunite with him or anything."

"Why didn't you tell me the other day?"

"I don't know. It's only now that I was thinking things over and I thought somebody should know. Especially with Earl being murdered."

"Do you still have those letters?"

"I do. I have them at home."

"What else did she say?"

"She asked whether I might be able to find out where Earl was. I know someone who works for the IRS and she asked me to see if my friend would somehow be able to find his address."

"And do you know if she's in contact with anybody else in her old community?"

Roslyn shook her head. "Not that I know of. I don't think so, but she could be."

"Denke, Roslyn. You've been very helpful."

"I just hope she didn't do anything foolish."

"Do you mind telling the police what you told us?"

"I'm not comfortable talking to them. I will if you think it's important."

"It might be and it might not be," Ettie said. "We'll let the detective know what you told us."

She shook her head. "I don't want to get Betsy into trouble. Maybe I shouldn't have come here."

When Roslyn left, Ettie and Elsa-May hurried down to the road to call Crowley and tell him what they had learned.

"We had better go back and visit Betsy. I'll have someone from the station call the hospital and find out what shifts she's on. It's better if we can catch her at home.

Half an hour later, Crowley was standing at their front door.

"I've just learned that Betsy is finishing a shift in half an hour. If we leave now we can catch her at home. Unless you ladies have something better to do this evening?"

"This takes priority," Ettie said.

Elsa-May said, "Doesn't Detective Kelly want to speak with her?"

"I ran it by him and he's following other leads."

"I don't think we'll find out too much if you're there with us," Ettie said to Crowley.

"I'm just the driver; you ladies can talk with her by yourselves, and I'll wait in the car."

* * *

Ettie and Elsa-May knocked on Betsy's door. They didn't have to wait long before the door opened and Betsy stood there in her scrubs.

"This is a nice surprise. Come inside."

The sisters walked inside and followed Betsy to her small living room.

"Is this about Earl?" Betsy asked.

"Yes, it is."

"I don't see how I can help you. What is it you want to know?"

"We heard from your old pen pal that you were talking a lot about Earl in your letters."

"Yes, that's right."

Elsa-May asked, "And why was that?"

"When I ran away with him, it changed the course of my life. It took me some time to get my life back together and I was just curious to find out where he ended up."

"What do you know about a drug called meperidine?" Ettie noticed Betsy's eyes flicking about as though she didn't know where to look.

"It's a fairly common drug, commonly known as

demerol. Of course, I've heard of it."

"Common, but only available by prescription," Elsa-May pointed out.

Ettie continued, "Betsy, this is how I think things played out. You ran into a man, a pharmaceutical salesman, Michael Skully, and you forged some kind of a friendship. Soon you found out you had an acquaintance in common and that was Earl Fuller. He was an enemy to both of you. You wanted to pay him back for what he'd done to you, and Michael simply wanted him out of the way for the sake of his girlfriend."

A tear trickled down Betsy's face. "We didn't kill him."

Ettie leaned forward, "Tell me what happened, Betsy—the truth this time."

Betsy breathed heavily. "I need a drink of water."

The elderly widows waited patiently for Betsy, and when she came back, she began her story, "We had it all planned out, but we didn't end up killing him. Earlier that evening, I put meperidine in Earl's drink, wanting him dead. I got it from Michael. It was supposed to kill him but he only drank half of it. I tried to get him to drink the rest, but he said he had things to do that night. He mumbled about someone sending him a note and trying to make things right." She wiped another tear from her eye.

"Go on," Elsa-May said.

"I didn't know what to do. I called Michael in a panic telling him that he didn't drink all of it and Michael suggested that we follow him and finish him off." She looked down into her hands that were fidgeting in her lap. "All this is so awful."

Elsa-May said softly. "Go on. Then what happened?"

"We followed him to a house and then it was dark and we couldn't see him. We knew he hadn't gone into the house. We got out of the car and walked closer, and then we found his body there with a rope around his neck and he was dead. We got out of there quick. We ran back to the car and tried to drive away but the battery in the car was dead."

"And then you got out of the car and walked away while Michael stayed there and tried to start the car."

"Yes, how did you know?"

"Santa Claus told me."

"What Ettie means is that a man dressed as Santa Claus was in the street, and he heard various car doors opening and closing."

"Oh. Will they arrest me?"

"I think your best chance is to come with us and turn yourself in. Tell them what you know and what your part in it was."

"Otherwise, this will haunt you forever," Elsa-May added.

"Okay. I'll do what you say. I've had enough trouble in my life. I've learned it's best to face things rather than run away from them. I've wished I could turn back the clock."

Ettie and Elsa-May accompanied Betsy out to Crowley's car and he drove them to the police station.

When Betsy was taken into an interview room, the sisters waited for her while Crowley disappeared somewhere in response to a call on his cell phone.

As they sat, Elsa-May whispered to Ettie, "Do you believe that she didn't do it?"

"She tried to kill him. I don't think she'll get off lightly."

"That's not what I asked. How do we know what she's saying is the truth?"

"I don't suppose we do. But, if what's she's saying is right, who finished him off outside our *haus?*"

"Ettie, didn't she say there was a rope around his neck?"

Ettie nodded. "That's right and by the time I got there just behind Crowley, there was nothing around that anyone could've strangled him with."

"So, we have a missing piece of rope?"

"It appears we do."

A little while later, Detective Kelly came and sat beside them. "Good evening, ladies."

"Hello, Detective Kelly. Were you interviewing Betsy Stoll?"

"I wasn't directly, but I heard what she had to

say."

"Will you arrest her?"

He shook his head. "Not at this stage. We still have to determine if she's telling the truth or trying to save Michael and herself from a murder charge. It works against us if we arrest people without proper evidence."

"While Ettie and I've been sitting here, we realized that Betsy mentioned that there was a rope around Earl's neck."

Ettie added, "And I reached the body just behind Ronald, and there was nothing around his neck. I remember Ronald stating that there was nothing around that he could've been strangled with. It's a little fuzzy now, but I assume that Ronald must've seen marks on his neck or something like that."

Kelly scratched his head. "Yes, you're right. I'd thought of that. Where did that rope get to? We need to find it. According to the coroner, he was strangled with a rope. There were fibers embedded into his neck and the wounds were consistent with a corded nylon rope. It seems Betsy was telling the truth about that."

"Perhaps you should talk to Santa Claus again?" Ettie asked. "To ask if he saw a rope."

Detective Kelly stuck his nose in the air. "The man's not right in the head, Mrs. Smith, we can't really rely on anything he says. There'd be no point."

"Well that might be true, but don't you think it would be interesting to hear what he said about a rope?"

"I'll go over the evidence and make a determination whether I have enough to arrest Skully and possibly Betsy as his accomplice. Attempted murder is a serious felony. Since Betsy's come forward first, she'll be better off than Skully."

"Will Betsy be able to go home tonight?"

"Later. And we'll need to search your house."

"Of course, any time," Ettie said.

"I'll get a team out there tomorrow. We've gone right through your garden and your front yard."

"Do you mind if Ettie and I visit Santa?"

"It's a free country." Kelly was then called away by Ronson, the young detective who had been at the sisters' house on Christmas Day.

Ettie and Elsa-May stared at each other again.

"It seems like they'll be charged for attempted murder," Ettie said.

Elsa-May sighed. "That's what they did. Unless, they were lying and they really did it. Attempted murder's a better charge than murder."

"Well, she didn't have to tell us what she told us. And I'd guess she wouldn't have said anything if she were guilty of actually murdering him."

"Don't worry, Ettie, Kelly said she'd get off lighter for coming forward."

Crowley approached them. "I'll take you ladies home now."

"But what about Betsy?"

"An officer will drive her home. She'll be okay. They won't keep her too much longer. They're preparing a statement for her to sign."

"Thank you, Ronald. It's been very good to have your help throughout this whole thing, and I know

Myra appreciates your support."

Crowley smiled somewhat wistfully, and gave a small nod.

Chapter 21

The next day, Ettie and Elsa-May sat in front of Santa Claus in the day room of the facility where he lived.

"I was hoping you'd come back to visit me, but I didn't think it'd be so soon. Where's Ronald?"

"He couldn't come today. We just have a couple of questions. We won't keep you long."

"I've got all the time in the world, until next Christmas."

Ettie cleared her throat. "When you found the man outside our house, did you see a rope around his neck?"

"I thought the man was drunk so I gave him a bit of a nudge and when he didn't move I put my head against his chest to see if he was breathing. He wasn't. After that, I put my two fingers on his neck to see if there was a pulse." He shook his head. "There was no pulse, and no rope around his neck."

"Thank you, Santa, for clearing something up."

Elsa-May asked, "Can you tell us everything you saw and heard from the moment you entered the street?"

"Didn't I tell you this already?" His blue eyes twinkled as he stared from one sister to the other.

"Yes, but our memory is nowhere near as good as yours."

His rosy cheeks puffed out as he smiled. "Mind if I close my eyes while I talk? I remember better that way."

"Go ahead," Elsa-May said. "We'll sit here and listen."

"I reached the dark street…"

"How did you get there?" Elsa-May asked, which made Santa jolt and open his eyes.

Ettie dug her in the ribs. "You said you'd sit quietly."

"Yes, sorry." Elsa-May turned to Santa. "Go on."

He nodded and said, "A taxi took me to the end of the street. I went on from there."

"Very good," Elsa-May said with a nod while

Ettie frowned at her when because she'd caused Santa to open his eyes again.

Santa closed his eyes once more. "I got out of the taxi, paid the driver and he went on his way. I had my donations tin in my hand and I made my way up the street. A car drove past me and the driver was a man, Michael Skully…"

"But you didn't know him before that night, before you overheard him tell the police his name?"

"Santa Claus knows everyone."

"Yes, of course," Ettie said. "Sorry for interrupting, continue."

"Michael slowed down and had a good look at me and then he kept going. Later the police found him in the car across the street."

"Could there have been anyone else in the car with him?" Ettie asked knowing now that there was.

"I'm almost certain there was because I heard the two car doors open and close while I was at the first house in the street. Then a few minutes after that, they opened and closed again, and then I heard the car try to start but it wouldn't kick over. After that another door opened and closed."

"Did you see or hear anything else?"

"Only a distant buggy."

"How distant?" Elsa-May asked.

"It was hard to tell, but the clip-clopping reminded me I was in Amish country."

"It must've been close by because the snow would've muffled the sound to some degree," Elsa-May said to Ettie.

"Did you hear any other cars?" Ettie asked.

"No."

"Then what happened?"

"I approached your house, found the dead man, and I've told you the rest already."

"There's nothing you forgot to mention? Because we didn't hear about the buggy the last time we spoke."

"No. There's nothing else."

* * *

The sisters weren't home long when they got a surprise visit from Myra.

She sat down on the couch looking terribly distressed.

"Did Crowley tell you the latest?" Elsa-May asked.

"Yes. He told me that Michael and Betsy had some involvement. I didn't even know that Michael knew Betsy."

"I don't think there was anything beyond a friendship. So don't be concerned."

Myra nodded. "I'm not thinking about anything like that. I just don't like to think that Michael might have done something wrong."

"The police said they want to come here to search the place. They're looking for a missing rope that Earl was strangled with."

A tear trickle down Myra's cheek. "I have such terrible trouble choosing men. What did Betsy tell you?"

Ettie told Myra everything they were told by Betsy, and then everything that Santa had told them.

Myra shook her head. “I still can’t believe it. I still can’t believe Michael would do such a thing.” Myra burst into tears.

Ettie looked over at Elsa-May wondering what to do. She then sat closer and patted Myra on her back.

Myra looked up at them through tear-filled eyes. “I was the one who took the rope!”

Chapter 22

"What?" Ettie asked, trying to make sense of Myra's words.

"How could you have taken the rope, Myra, if you were in the house the whole time?" Elsa-May asked as she leaned across and offered Myra a white handkerchief.

Myra unfolded it and blew her nose. "I was on my way to make a call when I got stuck talking to people, and then Crowley came and I was talking to him. I slipped outside for a moment to make that call to postpone the talk I was going to have with Earl."

"Did you talk to Earl?"

"No. His phone went straight to his message service. Anyway, then I saw a body, and, looking closer I saw it was Earl. I heard a car trying to start and I was upset to see that it was Michael's car. In the light coming out from the window, I saw a rope. Then I heard someone whistling Silent

Night and coming my way. The whistling was growing louder. I knew I had to do something. My first thought was to help Michael, since Earl was already dead. I pulled the rope off his neck and ran around the side of the house."

"Where is the rope?" Elsa-May asked.

"I threw it under the house, around the side. Then I came back inside by the back door so no one would see I was gone. I sat back down just as Ronald brought me over a drink. I guess that's why he thought I was there, in the house, the whole time."

Elsa-May shook her head. "Why involve yourself like that, Myra?"

"I don't know. I was in shock and everything was happening so fast. I thought Michael killed him and I was trying to help him. Well, not help him exactly but make things not as bad for him."

"Is that a car?" Elsa-May said pushing herself to her feet.

Ettie got to the window before Elsa-May. "Here they are to search the house."

"I suppose they'll find the rope now with my prints on it, or DNA or whatever. I'll have to tell them what happened."

After Myra told the officers about the rope, they had her show them where it was and then had her go to the station to make a statement.

It wasn't long before Ettie and Elsa-May sat in their living room, still stunned by Myra's confession and being consoled by Crowley, who had been told the news.

"It seems everyone had a hand in Earl Fuller's murder," Ettie said.

"Well, covering it up and intending to murder him. We still don't know who did the final deed. He was by no means a popular man," Crowley said.

Elsa-May said, "What about Earl's brother? Maybe he holds some clues."

"We checked into the story he gave us at the funeral and Earl had visited him on three occasions in the past few months. It seems Wayne's story about his brother visiting him checks out."

"But you don't know whether he's telling the truth about what Earl told him."

"You still think this is all about Myra, Ettie?" Crowley asked.

"I don't know," Ettie said. "I did, to begin with."

"I'll tell you what. How would the two of you feel about visiting Wayne? Unless you'd rather not go to a prison?"

"We've done it before," Elsa-May said. "I think we should do that. What do you think, Ettie?"

"We'll visit him," she said.

* * *

Kelly was able to pull some strings and get the sisters in to visit Wayne the next day. Crowley drove them there.

"Are you nervous?" Crowley asked when they were getting out of the car.

"No, we'll be okay."

"At least he knows us."

Ettie and Elsa-May walked up to the visitors'

section through huge gates topped with rolled barbed wire. They'd been to the maximum-security prison before. They knew they would have to wait until all the visitors were together and all had gone through their security procedures. The sisters, along with a group of twenty other visitors, were asked to stand in a straight line. Then a dog was sent along the row, sniffing them. Ettie was glad she didn't have any of that pork on her from the night before. She held a straight face while thinking about how things would play out if she'd had some meat hidden on her.

After the dog had done his bit, the visitors filed through the metal detector one by one after they'd taken off their shoes.

"Please take off your hat," one of the officers said to Ettie.

The man towered over Ettie by a good ten inches and his face was hard. "This is a prayer *kapp* and I'll not take it off."

Deep lines appeared across his forehead. "If you don't take it off, I can't let you through."

His voice had increased in volume and Ettie could see everyone staring at her.

Ettie stood as tall as she could and lifted her head high. No one would make her take off her *kapp!* "I've been here before and they let me leave it on." She stared up at the guard.

Elsa-May, standing in line behind her, said, "That's right! They let us through last time and they said nothing about our prayer *kapps.*"

He stared at them both. "Okay," he finally said. "Do you have anything to declare? Any drugs, phones, or valuables?"

"No."

They let Ettie through and Elsa-May came after her. They sat down, placed their boots back on, and joined again with the crowd. Soon the visitors were taken single file into a large area where they sat in booths as directed, and waited to see the prisoners.

"I thought we were going to get thrown out back there, Ettie."

"Me too, but they let us through last time."

"I know."

"Here he comes," Ettie said.

Wayne snorted and laughed when he saw them sitting there waiting for him. When he sat in front of them, he said, "I didn't know it was you two. They just told me I had a visitor."

"Here we are," Elsa-May said.

"We're here to ask you some questions. I hope you don't mind."

"I haven't got anything better to do."

"Is it true that your brother, Earl …. You take over, Ettie. I just forgot what I was going to say."

"Wayne, did Earl tell you that my daughter, Myra, stole his business ideas?"

"Yes, that's what he said." He laughed. "Don't look so worried, Mrs. Smith. I never could believe a thing he said."

"So, you think he was lying?"

"Most likely. He certainly wouldn't tell me that he stole someone's idea. Come to think of it, he might, just to brag." Wayne laughed again.

Ettie immediately felt better. "Do you have any idea who might have killed him?"

"If I was Naomi, I reckon I'd want him dead. Then again, he misled so many women."

"Did he speak of anyone? A woman?" Elsa-May asked.

"Only Myra. He had a fixation on Myra. I don't know if they were friends or what, but that's all he'd want to talk about. He was complaining about her."

"You'd left the community before he ran away with Betsy, is that right?"

"Yes. I remember I was at his wedding and I left the community a few weeks after that—it might have been months."

"And you mentioned other women. Can you name any of them?"

He sneered. "I didn't take too much notice what my brother was doing. All I know is what I told you. Mind you, I can't say for certain that Betsy wasn't the only one, but it's my best guess that she wasn't. I remember thinking that I was surprised that he married Naomi because I was certain he had his eyes on someone else. And, from memory, it wasn't Betsy."

"Thank you. You've been a great help. Someone said your brother was going to look after you when you got out?"

"Don't worry about me, Mrs. Smith. I've got a job lined up already. I'm not coming back to this place and I've made myself that as a promise."

"If you ever need any help, Elsa-May and I will do what we can."

"Thank you. I appreciate your offer."

When he stood up, he put his arms out and a nearby guard slapped the cuffs back on his wrists. He gave them a little smile as he was being led away.

Ettie fought back a tear at the man being treated in that way. He'd made bad choices along the way and he was paying for his crimes. Ettie looked over at Elsa-May.

"Did you have to say that, Ettie?"

"What?"

"He might turn up on our doorstep expecting to stay."

“No he wouldn’t. If he did, though, we’d find a way to help him.”

“I know. Let’s go,” Elsa-May said as she pushed herself to her feet.

Chapter 23

That night after the visit to the prison, Ettie tossed and turned. It was then that she decided to read Betsy's letters from Roslyn. She lit the lantern beside her, and walked over to the box of letters that had been sitting on her dresser for days. After she had pulled out a handful, she slipped back between the sheets. After reading four long letters, she fell asleep.

"That's it!" Ettie sat bolt upright in bed when all the pieces of the murder puzzle finally fitted. She could see from the gentle light outside that it was early in the morning. The sound of Elsa-May snoring loudly told her just how early it was. Ettie giggled at the rhythmic sounds.

Earl's murder had occurred with a gathering at her house, so the best thing to do, Ettie figured, was to have another gathering at her house to reveal the identity of the killer. She would run her idea past Detective Kelly when she reckoned he'd be awake.

That afternoon, their small living room was crowded once again. As well as Crowley, there was Detective Kelly, along with Santa, Myra, Michael Skully, the pen pal Roslyn, and Naomi Fuller. Moses Stoll was there with his daughter, Betsy, who was now on speaking terms with him.

Detective Kelly stood up. "I want to thank everyone for being here tonight. Most of you were present when Earl Fuller was murdered. I know we all want this case to be solved. Is there anyone here who would like to make a confession before we start?" Kelly's eyes swept across the silent crowd. "Very well. I'll hand this over to Mrs. Smith."

Ettie walked over to where Kelly had been standing. "Thank you, Detective. Myra, you admit to taking away the rope from Earl's neck, but did you reach him before or after he was dead?"

"He was dead," Myra insisted.

Ettie turned to Michael. "Michael, you say..."

Michael cut across her. "I don't say anything without my lawyer present."

Ettie tugged on the string of her prayer *kapp.*

"Myra claims she saw your car out front, Michael, and that's why she hid the rope from around Earl's neck. It seems your… Myra, thought you capable of murder."

"Mother!"

"Hush, Myra!" Ettie snapped back. "Betsy, you admit to being in a plot with Michael to murder Earl."

Betsy hung her head, while her father put his arm around her.

"She was tested by *Gott* for many years," Moses said in his daughter's defense.

"Or, could Moses have killed Earl, finally taking revenge for his daughter?" Ettie suggested.

Moses shook his head and looked down.

Ettie continued, "Moses, you claim to have seen Naomi go outside shortly before Santa came inside. Naomi, you claim the same about Moses. Which out of the two of you is mistaken, or perhaps covering up for someone else? Perhaps you both saw someone go outside and that person could have been Myra. She might have put on her black coat which would’ve covered her bright dress.”

Naomi and Moses stared at each other.

“Santa.”

“Yes?”

“Thank you for being here tonight. You saw Michael Skully drive past and look at you.”

“Yes.”

“Santa, you told me that you heard two car doors open and close while you were at the first house in the street. Then a few minutes after that, they opened and closed again, and then you heard the car try to start but it wouldn’t kick over. Then you heard one door open and then shut. Which holds true to what Betsy said, that she got out of the car when it wouldn’t start. Which would’ve given Betsy enough time to go back and finish Earl off if he wasn’t yet dead.”

Santa nodded.

Betsy stood up. “I didn’t! I went the other way. I just wanted to get out of there before I got blamed for anything. Michael told me to go and save myself.”

"Betsy, why did you think Earl was already dead when he was lying down?"

"Michael told me he was."

"Being a nurse, didn't you think to check on him yourself?"

"I was scared."

"Perhaps Earl wasn't dead at that time and when you left, Michael came back and finished him off?"

Michael sprang to his feet. "I did no such thing."

Ettie held a hand in the air. "I'm far from finished."

Michael sat back down.

When Ettie continued talking, Betsy sat back down as well. "Santa, before you heard the two car doors open and shut, you heard the sound of a buggy?"

"That's right."

"Which brings me to why you're here tonight, Roslyn."

"I was wondering when you'd get around to me," Roslyn said with a girlish giggle.

"I put it to you that Earl promised to marry you

and then blindsided you by marrying Naomi."

A gasp sounded across the room and all eyes fell on Roslyn.

Ettie went on, "From the time he met you at your visit to the community, he sought you out, and then he kept you dangling on a string. He told you he was going to leave the community for you, but he married Naomi. After that, he explained he was forced to marry Naomi and then promised you he was going to leave her. But he left his marriage and ran away with Betsy instead of you."

Naomi and Betsy glared at Roslyn.

Ettie continued, "He jilted you, Roslyn, not once but twice."

Roslyn hung her head.

Detective Kelly said, "Hell hath no fury like a woman scorned."

Betsy stared at Roslyn. "Is what Ettie said true?"

Roslyn jumped to her feet. "It's all a bunch of lies. I don't have to stay here and listen to this."

"I think you do, Roslyn," Ettie said calmly. "You see, it's all there in your letters." She pointed at the box of letters. "You were subtly trying to gather information from your pen pal about Earl after your visit to the community. Not only that, but Wayne, Earl's brother, remembers Earl was keen on you."

"That doesn't mean I killed him."

Kelly stood up. "But the DNA evidence on the rope does." Kelly walked over to the box of letters, and from behind the box he pulled a plastic bag. Inside the clear bag, a blue nylon rope was evident. "You see, we have your DNA and prints in our system from when you were suspected of your mother's murder."

Again everyone gasped and stared at Roslyn.

Kelly kept going, "This is the same rope that Myra pulled from the victim after he was killed."

"I thought you were my only friend, Roslyn," Betsy said in a small voice.

Her father tightened his arm around Betsy's shoulders.

Detective Kelly pressed a button on his phone and within seconds a flurry of police cars pulled up in front of the house.

Kelly took Roslyn by the arm and she was placed in handcuffs. Betsy and Michael were then arrested for attempted murder.

Moses stood in the doorway of Ettie's house watching his daughter be led away. "I should've been able to prevent this somehow."

"*Nee,* Moses. You couldn't have done anything."

Crowley stepped forward. "Betsy gave herself up. I think you'll be surprised how easy they are on her. This is her first offense, which helps as well."

"I see you two are now talking," Elsa-May said to Moses.

"Betsy wants to come home after all this time. She's prepared to take whatever the bishop tells her to do. She'll stand up and confess her sins in front of the congregation."

Ettie patted him on his shoulder. "Out of bad things, sometimes good things come."

He gave a little smile and nodded.

Kelly came back into the house. "Michael and Betsy will most likely get bail tomorrow. I can't say whether Roslyn will or not. Good job, Mrs. Smith."

"It was thanks to those letters."

"I wonder how she came and went without anyone seeing her?" Elsa-May asked.

Ettie turned and looked at Naomi who was still sitting on the couch as though she had been stunned.

"Naomi, I'm sorry to put you through all of this."

"It's good to put it all behind me, once and for all. I'm glad I know what happened to him."

Ettie looked at Santa. "Did you hear anything else that would explain how Roslyn did this without anyone seeing her? You were in the street; the only car you saw was Michael's."

He stroked his long white beard. "She had to have been in his car."

"Yes! She must've driven here with Earl."

"That must be how it happened," Santa said nodding.

Detective Kelly said, "I'll see what I can find out. We'll have to have all the nitty gritty details work out before we go to court. Hopefully, we'll have some confessions by then."

Chapter 24

It was a week later that Crowley and Kelly visited Elsa-May and Ettie.

Elsa-May sat on her favorite chair and Ettie was on her couch, while the two men were sitting on wooden chairs opposite the couch. As always, there was hot tea and cake.

"How's Myra?" Ettie asked Crowley.

"She's doing a lot better."

From the look on his face, Ettie knew they were seeing more of one another and she was pleased. If Myra was never going to return to the community, she couldn't think of a better man for her daughter than Crowley.

"Tell us what details you've found out?" Elsa-May asked Kelly.

Kelly nodded while finishing a mouthful of chocolate cake. When he'd picked up his full teacup, he began, "Michael wrote those Christmas invitations to give Myra an alibi while he and

Betsy killed the man. What Michael didn't realize was that Myra had invited Earl to your house, Mrs. Smith. That really made things awkward for him."

When Snowy heard Kelly's voice, he lifted his head up. He left his bed in the corner and tried to jump on the detective's lap, but his legs were too short.

"Oh, dear. I'm sorry, Detective," Elsa-May said as Kelly was trying to balance his full teacup while he was being pawed at.

"Put him outside, Elsa-May," Ettie said, not wanting Kelly to spill his tea everywhere.

Elsa-May scooped Snowy up and closed him in her room and then joined them once more. "I'm sorry, go ahead. Did I miss anything?"

"No, we were waiting for you. As I was saying, Betsy called Earl to have a drink with her at a local bar—one of the rare establishments open on Christmas Day. She slipped the Demerol to him, but he only drank half of a lethal dose and then he left. Keen to finish what she'd started, she called Michael, her accomplice, to tell him that she'd been unable to persuade Earl to stay longer and he hadn't had enough of the poison to kill him. Right then he saw a text message on his phone from Myra asking him whether he was coming to her mother's house and telling him that she'd asked Earl there too. Bingo! Now they suddenly knew where Earl was headed. Michael collected Betsy from the bar and together they traveled to your house, Mrs. Smith."

Crowley added, "Meanwhile, Earl had collected Roslyn for a date. He told her he had to stop in at someone's house and he wouldn't be long. She told us she'd had enough of his philandering and empty promises and he was behaving as though he was drunk and she took that to mean he'd come to her from meeting a woman for some drinks. Which was true, but he wasn't drunk, he'd been poisoned. As soon as he got out of the car, Roslyn grabbed a rope that was around a box in his back seat."

Ettie rubbed her chin. "Roslyn got out of the car and strangled him with the rope?"

"She said she thought he was seeing other

women. Which he was; he was going to speak with Myra, who he was stalking and harassing."

Elsa-May reached forward and took a piece of cake. "After all this time, Earl had kept a relationship going with Roslyn."

Crowley said, "As you put it the other night, Ettie, he'd kept her dangling on a string for years, it seems."

Ettie said, "Then she left on foot after but not before wiping the car of all evidence that she was ever there? She slipped away without being seen, just seconds before Santa arrived in the street."

"Yes. That sums it up nicely." Kelly nodded.

"All's well that ends well," Crowley said. "I'm just glad that Santa Claus didn't have anything to do with the murder."

Kelly shook his head. "I didn't think for a moment the harmless old man had anything to do with it."

"I feel sad for him thinking he's Santa Claus," Crowley said.

Ettie smiled as she pictured the dear jolly old

man. "He seems happy enough. I don't think you need to feel sorry or sad for him."

Kelly frowned at Ettie. "Mrs. Smith, the man thinks he's the real Santa Claus. How can you say not to feel sorry for him?"

Crowley laughed. "Maybe he *is* the real Santa and he's been telling the truth all along and no one will listen to him."

Elsa-May looked at Ettie. "Don't say it, Ettie."

"Why not? I was telling Elsa-May earlier that I know he couldn't be the real Santa Claus because his elves would've gotten him back to the North Pole."

Elsa-May shook her head and looked across at the detectives. "See what I have to put up with?"

Whether therefore ye eat, or drink,
or whatsoever ye do, do all to the glory of God.
1 Corinthians 10:31

* * * * * * * * * * * * * *

Thank you for your interest in

'Amish Christmas Mystery'

Ettie Smith Amish Mysteries Book 10

For Samantha Price's New Release alerts, join Samantha's email list at www.samanthapriceauthor.com

Other Christmas Books by Samantha Price

Marry by Christmas

Amish Christmas Baby Gone

Other books in:

Ettie Smith Amish Mysteries

Book 1

Secrets Come Home

Book 2

Amish Murder

When a former Amish woman, Camille Esh, is murdered, the new detective in town is frustrated that no one in the Amish community will speak to him. The detective reluctantly turns to Ettie Smith for help. Soon after Ettie agrees to see what she can find out, the dead woman's brother, Jacob, is arrested for the murder. To prove Jacob's innocence, Ettie delves into the mysterious and secretive life of Camille Esh, and uncovers one secret after another.

Will Ettie be able to find proof that Jacob is innocent, even though the police have DNA evidence against him, and documentation that proves he's guilty?

Can Ettie uncover the real murderer amongst the many people who had reasons to want Camille dead?

Book 3:

Murder in the Amish Bakery

When Ettie has problems with her bread sinking in the middle, she turns to her friend, Ruth Fuller, who owns the largest Bakery in town.

When Ruth and Ettie discover a dead man in Ruth's Bakery with a knife in his back, Ruth is convinced the man was out to steal her bread recipe.

It was known that the victim, Alan Avery, was one of the three men who were desperate to get their hands on Ruth's bread secrets.

When it's revealed that Avery owed money all over town, the local detective believes he was after the large amount of cash that Ruth banks weekly.

Why was Alan Avery found with a Bible clutched in his hand? And what did it have to do with a man who was pushed down a ravine twenty years earlier?

Book 4

Amish Murder Too Close

Elderly Amish woman, Ettie Smith, finds a body outside her house. Everything Ettie thought she knew about the victim is turned upside down when she learns the dead woman was living a secret life. As the dead woman had been wearing an engagement ring worth close to a million dollars, the police must figure out whether this was a robbery gone wrong. When an Amish man falls under suspicion, Ettie has no choice but to find the real killer.

What information about the victim is Detective Kelly keeping from Ettie?

When every suspect appears to have a solid alibi, will Ettie be able to find out who murdered the woman, or will the Amish man be charged over the murder?

Book 5

Amish Quilt Shop Mystery

Amish woman, Bethany Parker, finally realizes her dream of opening her own quilt shop. Yet only days after the grand opening, when she invites Ettie Smith to see her store, they discover the body of a murdered man. At first Bethany is concerned that the man is strangely familiar to her, but soon she has more pressing worries when she discovers her life is in danger. Bethany had always been able to rely on her friend, Jabez, but what are his true intentions toward her?

Book 6

Amish Baby Mystery

Ettie and her sister, Elsa-May, find an abandoned baby boy wrapped in an Amish quilt on their doorstep. Ettie searches for clues as to the baby's identity and finds a letter in the folds of the quilt. The letter warns that if they don't keep the baby hidden, his life will be in danger.

When the retired Detective Crowley stumbles onto their secret, they know they need to find the baby's mother fast.

Will Ettie and Elsa-May be able to keep the baby safe and reunite him with his parents before it's too late?

What does the baby have to do with a cold case kidnapping that happened years before?

Book 7

Betrayed

Book 8

Amish False Witness

Florence Lapp's house has burned down, and her gun is missing. She learns that Dustin, a young man she knows, has been accused of murder and her gun has been found in his car.

Small things don't add up, and Florence believes the young man is innocent. Suspecting that her young friend has been framed, she turns to her sisters, Ettie and Elsa-May, for help.

Spurred on by the announcement that Florence is staying at their house until the case is solved, Ettie and Elsa-May hurry to find the truth.

Dustin says that he had no knowledge of a gun and didn't know the murdered girl.

Ettie begins to wonder if Florence's judgment might be swayed by the fact that many years ago she had a close association with Dustin's grandfather.

How will Ettie help prove Dustin is innocent when all the evidence, including the DNA evidence, proves otherwise?

Book 9

Amish Barn Murders

Amish man, Thomas Strongberg, had fallen off a ladder and is found on the floor of the family barn. After another man is found dead in the same barn, the police begin investigating Thomas' death as a murder rather than an accident.

Thea Hersh was there on the day Thomas died and heard him have a disagreement with an *Englischer.* When Thea enlists the help of her friend, Austin, to investigate Thomas's death, they are arrested and thrown in jail.

From her prison cell, Thea refuses to talk to anyone, but Ettie Smith.

Can Ettie discover the mystery of the strange lights in the Strongberg barn at night? Were they related to the murders?

Ettie finds that Thomas had a huge secret, and more than one person would benefit from his death. Will she find the real killer in time to save Thea and her friend from long prison sentences?

Samantha Price loves to hear from her readers.

Connect with Samantha at:

samanthaprice333@gmail.com

http://www.twitter.com/AmishRomance

http://www.samanthapriceauthor.com

http://www.facebook.com/SamanthaPriceAuthor

Made in the USA
Coppell, TX
25 July 2020